DEEP WATERS

DEEP WATERS

W.W. JACOBS

AUTHOR OF
'NIGHT WATCHES'
'THE CASTAWAYS'
ETC.

WILDSIDE PRESS

TO

MY FRIEND

ARTHUR WAUGH

CONTENTS

ILLUSTRATIONS

Shareholders

Shareholders

A SAILORMAN — said the night-watch-man, musingly — a sailorman is like a fish, he is safest when 'e is at sea. When a fish comes ashore it is in for trouble, and so is a sailorman. One poor chap I knew 'ardly ever came ashore without getting married; and when he was found out there was no less than six wimmen in the court all taking away 'is character at once. And when he spoke up about Solomon the magistrate pretty near bit 'is 'ead off.

Then look at the trouble they get in with their money! They come ashore from a long trip, smelling of it a'most, and they go from port to port like a lord. Everybody has got their eye on that money—everybody except the sailorman, that is—and afore he knows wot's 'appened, and who 'as got it, he's looking

3

Shareholders

for a ship agin. When he ain't robbed of 'is money, he wastes it; and when 'e don't do either, he loses it.

I knew one chap who hid 'is money. He'd been away ten months, and, knowing 'ow easy money goes, 'e made up sixteen pounds in a nice little parcel and hid it where nobody could find it. That's wot he said, and p'r'aps 'e was right. All I know is, *he* never found it. I did the same thing myself once with a couple o' quid I ran acrost unexpected, on'y, unfortunately for me, I hid it the day afore my missus started 'er spring-cleaning.

One o' the worst men I ever knew for getting into trouble when he came ashore was old Sam Small. If he couldn't find it by 'imself, Ginger Dick and Peter Russet would help 'im look for it. Generally speaking they found it without straining their eyesight.

I remember one time they was home, arter being away pretty near a year, and when they was paid off they felt like walking gold-mines. They went about smiling all over with good-

Shareholders

temper and 'appiness, and for the first three days they was like brothers. That didn't last, of course, and on the fourth day Sam Small, arter saying wot 'e would do to Ginger and Peter if it wasn't for the police, went off by 'imself.

His temper passed off arter a time, and 'e began to look cheerful agin. It was a lovely morning, and, having nothing to do and plenty in 'is pocket to do it with, he went along like a schoolboy with a 'arf holiday.

He went as far as Stratford on the top of a tram for a mouthful o' fresh air, and came back to his favourite coffee-shop with a fine appetite for dinner. There was a very nice gentlemanly chap sitting opposite 'im, and the way he begged Sam's pardon for splashing gravy over 'im made Sam take a liking to him at once. Nicely dressed he was, with a gold pin in 'is tie, and a fine gold watch-chain acrost his weskit; and Sam could see he 'ad been brought up well by the way he used 'is knife and fork. He kept looking at Sam in a thoughtful kind o' way,

5

and at last he said wot a beautiful morning it was, and wot a fine day it must be in the country. In a little while they began to talk like a couple of old friends, and he told Sam all about 'is father, wot was a clergyman in the country, and Sam talked about a father of his as was living private on three 'undred a year.

"Ah, money's a useful thing," ses the man.

"It ain't everything," ses Sam. "It won't give you 'appiness. I've run through a lot in my time, so I ought to know."

"I expect you've got a bit left, though," ses the man, with a wink.

Sam laughed and smacked 'is pocket. "I've got a trifle to go on with," he ses, winking back. "I never feel comfortable without a pound or two in my pocket."

"You look as though you're just back from a vy'ge," ses the man, looking at 'im very hard.

"I am," ses Sam, nodding. "Just back arter ten months, and I'm going to spend a bit o' money afore I sign on agin, I can tell you."

Shareholders

"That's wot it was given to us for," ses the man, nodding at him.

They both got up to go at the same time and walked out into the street together, and, when Sam asked 'im whether he might have the pleasure of standing 'im a drink, he said he might. He talked about the different kinds of drink as they walked along till Sam, wot was looking for a high-class pub, got such a raging thirst on 'im he hardly knew wot to do with 'imself. He passed several pubs, and walked on as fast as he could to the Three Widders.

"Do you want to go in there partikler?" ses the man, stopping at the door.

"No," ses Sam, staring.

" 'Cos I know a place where they sell the best glass o' port wine in London," ses the man.

He took Sam up two or three turnings, and then led him into a quiet little pub in a back street. There was a cosy little saloon-bar with nobody in it, and, arter Sam had 'ad two port wines for the look of the thing, he 'ad a pint

Shareholders

o' six-ale because he liked it. His new pal had
one too, and he 'ad just taken a pull at it and
wiped his mouth, when 'e noticed a little bill
pinned up at the back of the bar.

*"Lost, between — the Mint and — Tower
Stairs,"* he ses, léaning forward and reading
very slow, *"a gold—locket—set with—diamonds. Whoever will—return—the same to
—Mr. Smith—Orange Villa—Barnet—will
receive—thirty pounds—reward."*

" 'Ow much?" ses Sam, starting.

"Thirty pounds," ses the man. "Must be a
good locket. Where'd you get that?" he ses,
turning to the barmaid.

"Gentleman came in an hour ago," ses the
gal, "and, arter he had 'ad two or three drinks
with the guv'nor, he asks 'im to stick it up.
'Arf crying he was—said 'it 'ad belonged to his
old woman wot died."

She went off to serve a customer at the other
end of the bar wot was making little dents in
it with his pot, and the man came back and sat
down by Sam agin, and began to talk about

8

Shareholders

horse-racing. At least, he tried to, but Sam couldn't talk of nothing but that locket, and wot a nice steady sailorman could do with thirty pounds.

"Well, p'r'aps you'll find it," ses the man, chaffing-like. " 'Ave another pint."

Sam had one, but it only made 'im more solemn, and he got in quite a temper as 'e spoke about casuals loafing about on Tower Hill with their 'ands in their pockets, and taking gold lockets out of the mouths of hard-working sailormen.

"It mightn't be found yet," ses the man, speaking thoughtful-like. "It's wonderful how long a thing'll lay sometimes. Wot about going and 'aving a look for it?"

Sam shook his 'ead at fust, but arter turning the thing over in his mind, and 'aving another look at the bill, and copying down the name and address for luck, 'e said p'r'aps they might as well walk that way as anywhere else.

"Something seems to tell me we've got a chance," ses the man, as they stepped outside.

9

Shareholders

"It's a funny feeling and I can't explain it, but it always means good luck. Last time I had it an aunt o' mine swallered 'er false teeth and left me five 'undred pounds."

"There's aunts and aunts," ses Sam, grunting. "I 'ad one once, but if she had swallered *'er* teeth she'd ha' been round to me to help 'er buy some new ones. That's the sort *she* was."

"Mind!" ses the man, patting 'im on the shoulder, "if we do find this, I don't want any of it. I've got all I want. It's all for you."

They went on like a couple o' brothers arter that, especially Sam, and when they got to the Mint they walked along slow down Tower Hill looking for the locket. It was awkward work, because, if people saw them looking about, they'd 'ave started looking too, and twice Sam nearly fell over owing to walking like a man with a stiff neck and squinting down both sides of his nose at once. When they got as far as the Stairs they came back on the other side of the road, and they 'ad turned to go back agin

Shareholders

when a docker-looking chap stopped Sam's friend and spoke to 'im.

"I've got no change, my man," ses Sam's pal, pushing past him.

"I ain't begging, guv'nor," ses the chap, follering 'im up. "I'm trying to sell something."

"Wot is it?" ses the other, stopping.

The man looked up and down the street, and then he put his 'ead near them and whispered.

"Eh?" ses Sam's pal.

"Something I picked up," ses the man, still a-whispering.

Sam got a pinch on the arm from 'is pal that nearly made him scream, then they both stood still, staring at the docker.

"Wot is it?" ses Sam, at last.

The docker looked over his shoulder agin, and then 'e put his 'and in his trouser-pocket and just showed 'em a big, fat gold locket with diamonds stuck all over it. Then he shoved it back in 'is pocket, while Sam's pal was giving 'im a pinch worse than wot the other was.

"It's the one," he ses, in a whisper. "Let's 'ave another look at it," he ses to the docker.

The man fished it out of his pocket agin, and held on to it tight while they looked at it.

"Where did you find it?" ses Sam.

"Found it over there, just by the Mint," ses the man, pointing.

"Wot d'ye want for it?" ses Sam's pal.

"As much as I can get," ses the man. "I don't quite know 'ow much it's worth, that's the worst of it. Wot d'ye say to twenty pounds, and chance it?"

Sam laughed—the sort of laugh a pal 'ad once give him a black eye for.

"Twenty pounds!" he ses; "twenty pounds! 'Ave you gorn out of your mind, or wot? I'll give you a couple of quid for it."

"Well, it's all right, captin," ses the man, "there's no 'arm done. I'll try somebody else —or p'r'aps there'll be a big reward for it. I don't believe it was bought for a *'undred pounds.*"

He was just sheering off when Sam's pal

"FOUND IT OVER THERE, JUST BY THE MINT," SES THE MAN,
POINTING.

caught 'im by the arm and asked him to let 'im have another look at it. Then he came back to Sam and led 'im a little way off, whispering to 'im that it was the chance of a lifetime.

"And if you prefer to keep it for a little while and then sell it, instead of getting the reward for it, I dare say it would be worth a hundred pounds to you," 'e ses.

"I ain't got twenty pounds," ses Sam.

" 'Ow much 'ave you got?" ses his pal.

Sam felt in 'is pockets, and the docker came up and stood watching while he counted it. Altogether it was nine pounds fourteen shillings and tuppence.

"P'r'aps you've got some more at 'ome," ses his pal.

"Not a farthing," ses Sam, which was true as far as the farthing went.

"Or p'r'aps you could borrer some," ses his pal, in a soft, kind voice. "I'd lend it to you with pleasure, on'y I haven't got it with me."

Shareholders

Sam shook his 'ead, and at last, arter the docker 'ad said he wouldn't let it go for less than twenty, even to save 'is life, he let it go for the nine pounds odd, a silver watch-chain, two cigars wot Sam 'ad been sitting on by mistake, and a sheath-knife.

"Shove it in your pocket and don't let a soul see it," ses the man, handing over the locket. "I might as well give it away a'most. But it can't be 'elped."

He went off up the 'ill shaking his 'ead, and Sam's pal, arter watching him for a few seconds, said good-bye in a hurry and went off arter 'im to tell him to keep 'is mouth shut about it.

Sam walked back to his lodgings on air, as the saying is, and even did a little bit of a skirt-dance to a pianner-organ wot was playing. Peter and Ginger was out, and so was his landlady, a respectable woman as was minding the rest of 'is money for him, and when he asked 'er little gal, a kid of eleven, to trust 'im for some tin she gave 'im a lecture on wasting his

Shareholders

money instead wot took 'is breath away—all
but a word or two.

He got some of 'is money from his landlady
at eight o'clock, arter listening to 'er for 'arf
an hour, and then he 'ad to pick it up off of the
floor, and say "Thank you" for it.

He went to bed afore Ginger and Peter came
in, but 'e was so excited he couldn't sleep, and
long arter they was in bed he laid there and
thought of all the different ways of spending a
'undred pounds. He kept taking the locket
from under 'is piller and feeling it; then he
felt 'e must 'ave another look at it, and arter
coughing 'ard two or three times and calling
out to the other two not to snore—to see if
they was awake—he got out o' bed and lit the
candle. Ginger and Peter was both fast asleep,
with their eyes screwed up and their mouths
wide open, and 'e sat on the bed and looked at
the locket until he was a'most dazzled.

" 'Ullo, Sam!" ses a voice. "Wot 'ave you
got there?"

Sam nearly fell off the bed with surprise and

Shareholders

temper. Then 'e hid the locket in his 'and and
blew out the candle.

"Who gave it to you?" ses Ginger.

"You get off to sleep, and mind your own
bisness," ses Sam, grinding 'is teeth.

He got back into bed agin and laid there
listening to Ginger waking up Peter. Peter
woke up disagreeable, but when Ginger told
'im that Sam 'ad stole a gold locket as big as
a saucer, covered with diamonds, he altered 'is
mind.

"Let's 'ave a look at it," he ses, sitting up.

"Ginger's dreaming," ses Sam, in a shaky
voice. "I ain't got no locket. Wot d'you think
I want a locket for?"

Ginger got out o' bed and lit the candle
agin. "Come on!" he ses, "let's 'ave a look
at it. I wasn't dreaming. I've been awake all
the time, watching you."

Sam shut 'is eyes and turned his back to
them.

"He's gone to sleep, pore old chap," ses
Ginger. "We'll 'ave a look at it without wak-

ing 'im. You take that side, Peter! Mind you don't disturb 'im."

He put his 'and in under the bed-clo'es and felt all up and down Sam's back, very careful. Sam stood it for 'arf a minute, and then 'e sat up in bed and behaved more like a windmill than a man.

"Hold his 'ands," ses Ginger.

"Hold 'em yourself," ses Peter, dabbing 'is nose with his shirt-sleeve.

"Well, we're going to see it," ses Ginger, "if we have to make enough noise to rouse the 'ouse. Fust of all we're going to ask you per-lite; then we shall get louder and louder. *Show us the locket wot you stole, Sam!*"

"Show — us — the — diamond locket!" ses Peter.

"It's my turn, Peter," ses Ginger. "One, two, three. SHOW—US—TH'——"

"Shut up," ses Sam, trembling all over. "I'll show it to you if you stop your noise."

He put his 'and under his piller, but afore he showed it to 'em he sat up in bed and made 'em a little speech. He said 'e never wanted to see their faces agin as long as he lived, and why Ginger's mother 'adn't put 'im in a pail o' cold water when 'e was born 'e couldn't understand. He said 'e didn't believe that even a mother could love a baby that looked like a codfish with red 'air, and as for Peter Russet, 'e believed *his* mother died of fright.

"That'll do," ses Ginger, as Sam stopped to get 'is breath. "Are you going to show us the locket, or 'ave we got to shout agin?"

Sam swallered something that nearly choked 'im, and then he opened his 'and and showed it to them. Peter told 'im to wave it so as they could see the diamonds flash, and then Ginger waved the candle to see 'ow they looked that way, and pretty near set pore Sam's whiskers on fire.

They didn't leave 'im alone till they knew as much about it as he could tell 'em, and they both of 'em told 'im that if he took a reward of thirty pounds for it, instead of selling it for a 'undred, he was a bigger fool than he looked.

18

Shareholders

"I shall turn it over in my mind," ses Sam, sucking 'is teeth. "When I want your advice I'll ask you for it."

"We wasn't thinking of you," ses Ginger; "we was thinking of ourselves."

"*You!*" ses Sam, with a bit of a start. "Wot's it got to do with you?"

"Our share'll be bigger, that's all," ses Ginger.

"Much bigger," ses Peter. "I couldn't dream of letting it go at thirty. It's chucking money away. Why, we might get *two* 'undred for it. Who knows?"

Sam sat on the edge of 'is bed like a man in a dream, then 'e began to make a noise like a cat with a fish-bone in its throat, and then 'e tood up and let fly.

"Don't stop 'im, Peter," ses Ginger. "Let 'im go on; it'll do him good."

"He's forgot all about that penknife you picked up and went shares in," ses Peter. "I wouldn't be mean for *twenty* lockets."

"Nor me neither," ses Ginger. "But we

Shareholders

won't let 'im be mean—for 'is own sake. We'll 'ave our rights."

"Rights!" ses Sam. "Rights! You didn't find it."

"We always go shares if we find anything," ses Ginger. "Where's your memory, Sam?"

"But I didn't find it," ses Sam.

"No, you bought it," ses Peter, "and if you don't go shares we'll split on you—see? Then you can't sell it anyway, and perhaps you won't even get the reward. We can be at Orange Villa as soon as wot you can."

"Sooner," ses Ginger, nodding. "But there's no need to do that. If 'e don't go shares I'll slip round to the police-station fust thing in the morning."

"You know the way there all right," ses Sam, very bitter.

"And we don't want none o' your back-answers," ses Ginger. "Are you going shares or not?"

"Wot about the money I paid for it?" ses Sam, "and my trouble?"

Shareholders

Ginger and Peter sat down on the bed to talk it over, and at last, arter calling themselves a lot o' bad names for being too kind-'earted, they offered 'im five pounds each for their share in the locket.

"And that means you've got your share for next to nothing, Sam," ses Ginger.

"Some people wouldn't 'ave given you anything," ses Peter.

Sam gave way at last, and then 'e stood by making nasty remarks while Ginger wrote out a paper for them all to sign, because he said he had known Sam such a long time.

It was a'most daylight afore they got to sleep, and the fust thing Ginger did when he woke was to wake Sam up, and offer to shake 'ands with him. The noise woke Peter up, and, as Sam wouldn't shake 'ands with 'im either, they both patted him on the back instead.

They made him take 'em to the little pub, arter breakfast, to read the bill about the reward. Sam didn't mind going, as it 'appened, as he 'oped to meet 'is new pal there and tell 'im his troubles, but, though they stayed there some time, 'e didn't turn up. He wasn't at the coffee-shop for dinner, neither.

Peter and Ginger was in 'igh spirits, and, though Sam told 'em plain that he would sooner walk about with a couple of real pickpockets, they wouldn't leave 'im an inch.

"Anybody could steal it off of you, Sam," ses Ginger, patting 'im on the weskit to make sure the locket was still there. "It's a good job you've got us to look arter you."

"We must buy 'im a money-belt with a pocket in it," ses Peter.

Ginger nodded at 'im. "Yes," he ses, "that would be safer. And he'd better wear it next to 'is skin, with everything over it. I should feel more comfortable then."

"And wot about me?" says Sam, turning on 'im.

"Well, we'll take it in turns," ses Ginger. "You one day, and then me, and then Peter."

Shareholders

Sam gave way at last, as arter all he could
see it was the safest thing to do, but he 'ad
so much to say about it that they got fair sick
of the sound of 'is voice. They 'ad to go 'ome
for 'im to put the belt on; and then at seven
o'clock in the evening, arter Sam had 'ad two
or three pints, they had to go 'ome agin, 'cos
he was complaining of tight-lacing.

Ginger had it on next day and he went 'ome
five times. The other two went with 'im in
case he lost 'imself, and stood there making
nasty remarks while he messed 'imself up with
a penn'orth of cold cream. It was a cheap
belt, and pore Ginger said that, when they 'ad
done with it, it would come in handy for sand-
paper.

Peter didn't like it any better than the other
two did, and twice they 'ad to speak to 'im
about stopping in the street and trying to make
'imself more comfortable by wriggling. Sam
said people misunderstood it.

Arter that they agreed to wear it outside
their shirt, and even then Ginger said it

Shareholders

scratched 'im. And every day they got more and more worried about wot was the best thing to do with the locket, and whether it would be safe to try and sell it. The idea o' walking about with a fortune in their pockets that they couldn't spend a'most drove 'em crazy.

"The longer we keep it, the safer it'll be," ses Sam, as they was walking down Hounds-ditch one day.

"We'll sell it when I'm sixty," ses Ginger, nasty-like.

"Then old Sam won't be 'ere to have 'is share," ses Peter.

Sam was just going to answer 'em back, when he stopped and began to smile instead. Straight in front of 'im was the gentleman he 'ad met in the coffee-shop, coming along with another man, and he just 'ad time to see that it was the docker who 'ad sold him the locket, when they both saw 'im. They turned like a flash, and, afore Sam could get 'is breath, bolted up a little alley and disappeared.

Shareholders

"Wot's the row?" ses Ginger, staring.

Sam didn't answer 'im. He stood there struck all of a heap.

"Do you know 'em?" ses Peter.

Sam couldn't answer 'im for a time. He was doing a bit of 'ard thinking.

"Chap I 'ad a row with the other night," he ses, at last.

He walked on very thoughtful, and the more 'e thought, the less 'e liked it. He was so pale that Ginger thought 'e was ill and advised 'im to 'ave a drop o' brandy. Peter recommended rum, so to please 'em he 'ad both. It brought 'is colour back, but not 'is cheerfulness.

He gave 'em both the slip next morning; which was easy, as Ginger was wearing the locket, and, arter fust 'aving a long ride for nothing owing to getting in the wrong train, he got to Barnet.

It was a big place; big enough to 'ave a dozen Orange Villas, but pore Sam couldn't find one. It wasn't for want of trying neither.

Shareholders

He asked at over twenty shops, and the post-office, and even went to the police-station. He must ha' walked six or seven miles looking for it, and at last, 'arf ready to drop, 'e took the train back.

He 'ad some sausages and mashed potatoes with a pint o' stout at a place in Bishopsgate, and then 'e started to walk 'ome. The only comfort he 'ad was the thought of the ten pounds Ginger and Peter 'ad paid 'im; and when he remembered that he began to cheer up and even smile. By the time he got 'ome 'e was beaming all over 'is face.

"Where've you been?" ses Ginger.

"Enjoying myself by myself," ses Sam.

"Please yourself," ses Peter, very severe, "but where'd you ha' been if we 'ad sold the locket and skipped, eh?"

"You wouldn't 'ave enjoyed yourself by yourself then," ses Ginger. "Yes, you may laugh!"

Sam didn't answer 'im, but he sat down on 'is bed and 'is shoulders shook till Ginger lost his temper and gave him a couple o' thumps on the back that pretty near broke it.

"All right," ses Sam, very firm. "Now you 'ave done for yourselves. I 'ad a'most made up my mind to go shares; now you sha'n't 'ave a ha'penny."

Ginger laughed then. "Ho!" he ses, "and 'ow are you going to prevent it?"

"We've got the locket, Sam," ses Peter, smiling and shaking his 'ead at 'im.

"And we'll mind it till it's sold," ses Ginger.

Sam laughed agin, short and nasty. Then he undressed 'imself very slow and got into bed. At twelve o'clock, just as Ginger was dropping off, he began to laugh agin, and 'e only stopped when 'e heard Ginger getting out of bed to 'im.

He stayed in bed next morning, 'cos he said 'is sides was aching, but 'e laughed agin as they was going out, and when they came back he 'ad gorn.

We never know 'ow much we like anything till we lose it. A week arterwards, as Ginger

Shareholders

was being 'elped out of a pawnshop by Peter,
he said 'e would give all he 'adn't got for the
locket to be near enough to Sam to hear 'im
laugh agin.

Paying Off

Paving Off

Paying Off

MY biggest fault, said the night-watchman, gloomily, has been good-nature. I've spent the best part of my life trying to do my fellow-creeturs a good turn. And what do I get for it? If all the people I've helped was to come 'ere now there wouldn't be standing room for them on this wharf. 'Arf of them would be pushed overboard—and a good place for 'em, too.

I've been like it all my life. I was good-natured enough to go to sea as a boy because a skipper took a fancy to me and wanted my 'elp, and when I got older I was good-natured enough to get married. All my life I've given 'elp and advice free, and only a day or two ago one of 'em wot I 'ad given it to came round here with her 'usband and 'er two brothers and

Paying Off

'er mother and two or three people from the same street, to see her give me "wot for."

Another fault o' mine has been being sharp. Most people make mistakes, and they can't bear to see anybody as don't. Over and over agin I have showed people 'ow silly they 'ave been to do certain things, and told 'em wot I should ha' done in their place, but I can't remember one that ever gave me a "thank you" for it.

There was a man 'ere 'arf an hour ago that reminded me of both of these faults. He came in *a-purpose* to remind me, and 'e brought a couple o' grinning, brass-faced monkeys with 'im to see 'im do it. I was sitting on that barrel when he came, and arter two minutes I felt as if I was sitting on red-'ot cinders. He purtended he 'ad come in for the sake of old times and to ask arter my 'ealth, and all the time he was doing 'is best to upset me to amuse them two pore objecks 'e 'ad brought with 'im.

Capt'in Mellun is his name, and 'e was always a foolish, soft-'eaded sort o' man, and how he 'as kept 'is job I can't think. He used

Paying Off

to trade between this wharf and Bristol on a little schooner called the *Firefly,* and seeing wot a silly, foolish kind o' man he was, I took a little bit o' notice of 'im. Many and many a time when 'e was going to do something he'd ha' been sorry for arterwards I 'ave taken 'im round to the Bear's Head and stood 'im pint arter pint until he began to see reason and own up that I was in the right.

His crew was a'most as bad as wot he was, and all in one month one o' the 'ands gave a man ten shillings for a di'mond ring he saw 'im pick up, wot turned out to be worth fourpence, and another one gave five bob for a meerschaum pipe made o' chalk. When I pointed out to 'em wot fools they was they didn't like it, and a week arterwards, when the skipper gave a man in a pub 'is watch and chain and two pounds to hold, to show 'is confidence in 'im, and I told 'im exactly wot I thought of him, *'e* didn't like it.

"You're too sharp, Bill," he says, sneering like. "*My* opinion is that the pore man was

Paying Off

run over. He told me 'e should only be away five minutes. And he 'ad got an honest face: nice open blue eyes, and a smile that done you good to look at."

"You've been swindled," I ses, "and you know it. If I'd been done like that I should never hold up my 'ead agin. Why, a child o' five would know better. You and your crew all seem to be tarred with the same brush. You ain't fit to be trusted out alone."

I believe 'e told his 'ands wot I said; anyway, two bits o' coke missed me by 'arf an inch next evening, and for some weeks not one of 'em spoke a word to me. When they see me coming they just used to stand up straight and twist their nose.

It didn't 'urt me, o' course. I took no notice of 'em. Even when one of 'em fell over the broom I was sweeping with I took no notice of 'im. I just went on with my work as if 'e wasn't there.

I suppose they 'ad been in the sulks about a month, and I was sitting 'ere one evening get-

Paying Off

ting my breath arter a couple o' hours' 'ard work, when one of 'em, George Tebb by name, came off the ship and nodded to me as he passed.

"Evening, Bill," he ses.

"Evening," I ses, rather stiff.

"I wanted a word with you, Bill," he ses, in a low voice. "In fact, I might go so far as to say I want to ask you to do me a favour."

I looked at him so 'ard that he coughed and looked away.

"We might talk about it over a 'arf-pint," he ses.

"No, thank you," I ses. "I 'ad a 'arf-pint the day before yesterday, and I'm not thirsty."

He stood there fidgeting about for a bit, and then he puts his 'and on my shoulder.

"Well, come to the end of the jetty," he ses. "I've got something private to say."

I got up slow-like and followed 'im. I wasn't a bit curious. Not a bit. But if a man asks for my 'elp I always give it.

"It's like this," he ses, looking round careful,

Paying Off

"only I don't want the other chaps to hear because I don't want to be laughed at. Last week an old uncle o' mine died and left me thirty pounds. It's just a week ago, and I've already got through five of 'em, and besides that the number of chaps that want to borrow ten bob for a couple o' days would surprise you."

"I ain't so easy surprised," I ses, shaking my 'ead.

"It ain't safe with me," he ses; "and the favour I want you to do is to take care of it for me. I know it'll go if I keep it. I've got it locked up in this box. And if you keep the box I'll keep the key, and when I want a bit I'll come and see you about it."

He pulled a little box out of 'is pocket and rattled it in my ear.

"There's five-and-twenty golden goblins in there," he ses. "If you take charge of 'em they'll be all right. If you don't, I'm pretty certain I sha'n't 'ave one of 'em in a week or two's time."

At fust I said I wouldn't 'ave anything to do

Paying Off

with it, but he begged so 'ard that I began to alter my mind.

"You're as honest as daylight, Bill," he ses, very earnest. "I don't know another man in the world I could trust with twenty-five quid—especially myself. Now, put it in your pocket and look arter it for me. One of the quids in it is for you, for your trouble."

He slipped the box in my coat-pocket, and then he said 'is mind was so relieved that 'e felt like 'arf a pint. I was for going to the Bear's Head, the place I generally go to, because it is next door to the wharf, so to speak, but George wanted me to try the beer at another place he knew of.

"The wharf's all right," he ses. "There's one or two 'ands on the ship, and they won't let anybody run away with it."

From wot he said I thought the pub was quite close, but instead o' that I should think we walked pretty nearly a mile afore we got there. Nice snug place it was, and the beer was all right, although, as I told George Tebb, it

Paying Off

didn't seem to me any better than the stuff at the Bear's Head.

He stood me two 'arf-pints and was just going to order another, when 'e found 'e 'adn't got any money left, and he wouldn't hear of me paying for it, because 'e said it was his treat.

"We'll 'ave a quid out o' the box," he ses. "I must 'ave one to go on with, anyway."

I shook my 'ead at 'im.

"Only one," he ses, "and that'll last me a fortnight. Besides, I want to give you the quid I promised you."

I gave way at last, and he put his 'and in 'is trouser-pocket for the key, and then found it wasn't there.

"I must ha' left it in my chest," he ses. "I'll 'op back and get it." And afore I could prevent 'im he 'ad waved his 'and at me and gorn.

My fust idea was to go arter 'im, but I knew I couldn't catch 'im, and if I tried to meet 'im coming back I should most likely miss 'im

38

Paying Off

through the side streets. So I sat there with my pipe and waited.

I suppose I 'ad been sitting down waiting for him for about ten minutes, when a couple o' sailormen came into the bar and began to make themselves a nuisance. Big fat chaps they was, and both of 'em more than 'arf sprung. And arter calling for a pint apiece they began to take a little notice of me.

"Where d'you come from?" ses one of 'em.

" 'Ome," I ses, very quiet.

"It's a good place—'ome," ses the chap, shaking his 'ead. "Can you sing ' 'Ome, Sweet 'Ome'? You seem to 'ave got wot I might call a 'singing face.' "

"Never mind about my face," I ses, very sharp. "You mind wot you're doing with that beer. You'll 'ave it over in a minute."

The words was 'ardly out of my mouth afore 'e gave a lurch and spilt his pint all over me. From 'ead to foot I was dripping with beer, and I was in such a temper I wonder I didn't murder 'im; but afore I could move they

39

Paying Off

both pulled out their pocket-'ankerchers and started to rub me down.

"That'll do," I ses at last, arter they 'ad walked round me 'arf-a-dozen times and patted me all over to see if I was dry. "You get off while you're safe."

"It was my mistake, mate," ses the chap who 'ad spilt the beer.

"You get outside," I ses. "Go on, both of you, afore I put you out."

They gave one look at me, standing there with my fists clenched, and then they went out like lambs, and I 'eard 'em trot round the corner as though they was afraid I was following. I felt a little bit damp and chilly, but beer is like sea-water—you don't catch cold through it—and I sat down agin to wait for George Tebb.

He came in smiling and out 'o breath in about ten minutes' time, with the key in 'is 'and, and as soon as I told 'im wot had 'appened to me with the beer he turned to the landlord and ordered me six o' rum 'ot at once.

Paying Off

"Drink that up," he ses, 'anding it to me; "but fust of all give me the box, so as I can pay for it."

I put my 'and in my pocket. Then I put it in the other one, and arter that I stood staring at George Tebb and shaking all over.

"Wot's the matter? Wot are you looking like that for?" he ses.

"It must ha' been them two," I ses, choking. "While they was purtending to dry me and patting me all over they must 'ave taken it out of my pocket."

"Wot are you talking about?" ses George, staring at me.

"The box 'as gorn," I ses, putting down the 'ot rum and feeling in my trouser-pocket. "The box 'as gorn, and them two must 'ave taken it."

"Gorn!" ses George. "*Gorn!* My box with twenty-five pounds in, wot I trusted you with, gorn? Wot are you talking about? It can't be—it's too crool!"

He made such a noise that the landlord wot was waiting for 'is money, asked 'im wot he meant by it, and, arter he 'ad explained, I'm blest if the landlord didn't advise him to search me. I stood still and let George go through my pockets, and then I told 'im I 'ad done with 'im and I never wanted to see 'im agin as long as I lived.

"I dare say," ses George, "I dare say. But you'll come along with me to the wharf and see the skipper. I'm not going to lose five-and-twenty quid through your carelessness."

I marched along in front of 'im with my 'ead in the air, and when he spoke to me I didn't answer him. He went aboard the ship when we got to the wharf, and a minute or two arterwards 'e came to the side and said the skipper wanted to see me.

The airs the skipper gave 'imself was sickening. He sat down there in 'is miserable little rat-'ole of a cabin and acted as if 'e was a judge and I was a prisoner. Most of the 'ands 'ad squeezed in there too, and the things they advised George to do to me was remarkable.

"Silence!" ses the skipper. "Now, watch-

Paying Off

man, tèll me exactly 'ow this thing 'appened."

"I've told you once," I ses.

"I know," ses the skipper, "but I want you
to tell me again to see if you contradict yourself. I can't understand 'ow such a clever man
as you could be done so easy."

I thought I should ha' bust, but I kept my
face wonderful. I just asked 'im wot the men
was like that got off with 'is watch and chain
and two pounds, in case they might be the
same.

"That's different," he ses.

"Oh!" ses I. " 'Ow?"

"I lost my own property," he ses, "but you
lost George's, and 'ow a man like you, that's so
much sharper and cleverer than other people,
could be had so easy, I can't think. Why, a
child of five would ha' known better."

"A baby in arms would ha' known better,"
ses the man wot 'ad bought the di'mond ring.
" 'Ow *could* you 'ave been so silly, Bill? At
your time o' life. too!"

Paying Off

"That's neither 'ere nor there," ses the skipper. "The watchman has lost twenty-five quid belonging to one o' my men. The question is, wot is he going to do about it?"

"Nothing," I ses. "I didn't ask 'im to let me mind the box. He done it of 'is own free will. It's got nothing to do with me."

"Oh, hasn't it?" ses the skipper, drawing 'imself up. "I don't want to be too 'ard on you, but at the same time I can't let my man suffer. I'll make it as easy as I can, and I order you to pay 'im five shillings a week till the twenty-five pounds is cleared off."

I laughed; I couldn't 'elp it. I just stood there and laughed at 'im.

"If you don't," ses the skipper, "then I shall lay the facts of the case afore the guv'nor. Whether he'll object to you being in a pub a mile away, taking care of a box of gold while you was supposed to be taking care of the wharf, is his bisness. My bisness is to see that my man 'as 'is rights."

" 'Ear, 'ear!" ses the crew.

IN THE LIGHT OF THE LAMP I SAW THE DEAD WHITE FACE OF SAM
BULLET'S GHOST MAKING FACES AT ME.

Paying Off

"You please yourself, watchman," ses the skipper. "You're such a clever man that no doubt you could get a better job to-morrow. There must be 'eaps of people wanting a man like you. It's for you to decide. That's all I've got to say—five bob a week till pore George 'as got 'is money back, or else I put the case afore the guv'nor. *Wot* did you say?"

I said it agin, and, as 'e didn't seem to understand, I said it once more.

"Please yourself," 'e ses, when I 'ad finished. "You're an old man, and five bob a week can't be much loss to you. You've got nothing to spend it on, at your time o' life. And you've got a very soft job 'ere. Wot?"

I didn't answer 'im. I just turned round, and, arter giving a man wot stood in my way a punch in the chest, I got up on deck and on to the wharf, and said my little say all alone to myself, behind the crane.

I paid the fust five bob to George Tebb the next time the ship was up, and arter biting 'em over and over agin and then ringing 'em on the

Paying Off

deck 'e took the other chaps round to the **Bear's Head.**

"P'r'aps it's just as well it's 'appened," he ses. "Five bob a week for nearly two years ain't to be sneezed at. It's slow, but it's sure."

I thought 'e was joking at fust, but arter working it out in the office with a bit o' pencil and paper I thought I should ha' gorn crazy. And when I complained about the time to George 'e said I could make it shorter if I liked by paying ten bob a week, but 'e thought the steady five bob a week was best for both of us.

I got to 'ate the sight of 'im. Every week regular as clockwork he used to come round to me with his 'and out, and then go and treat 'is mates to beer with my money. If the ship came up in the day-time, at six o'clock in the evening he'd be at the wharf gate waiting for me; and if it came up at night she was no sooner made fast than 'e was over the side patting my trouser-pocket and saying wot a good job it was for both of us that I was in steady employment.

Week arter week and month arter month I

went on paying. I a'most forgot the taste o' beer, and if I could manage to get a screw o' baccy a week I thought myself lucky. And at last, just as I thought I couldn't stand it any longer, the end came.

I 'ad just given George 'is week's money— and 'ow I got it together that week I don't know —when one o' the chaps came up and said the skipper wanted to see me on board at once.

"Tell 'im if he wants to see me I'm to be found on the wharf," I ses, very sharp.

"He wants to see you about George's money," ses the chap. "I should go if I was you. My opinion is he wants to do you a good turn."

I 'ung fire for a bit, and then, arter sweeping up for a little while deliberate-like, I put down my broom and stepped aboard to see the skipper, wot was sitting on the cabin skylight purtending to read a newspaper.

He put it down when 'e see me, and George and the others, wot 'ad been standing in a little bunch for'ard, came aft and stood looking on.

47

Paying Off

"I wanted to see you about this money, watchman," ses the skipper, putting on 'is beastly frills agin. "O' course, we all feel that to a pore man like you it's a bit of a strain, and, as George ses, arter all you have been more foolish than wicked."

"Much more," ses George.

"I find that you 'ave now paid five bob a week for nineteen weeks," ses the skipper, "and George 'as been kind enough and generous enough to let you off the rest. There's no need for you to look bashful, George; it's a credit to you."

I could 'ardly believe my ears. George stood there grinning like a stuck fool, and two o' the chaps was on their best behaviour with their 'ands over their mouths and their eyes sticking out.

"That's all, watchman," ses the skipper; "and I 'ope it'll be a lesson to you not to neglect your dooty by going into public-'ouses and taking charge of other people's money when you ain't fit for it."

Paying Off

"I sha'n't try to do anybody else a kindness agin, if that's wot you mean," I ses, looking at 'im.

"No, you'd better not," he ses. "This partickler bit o' kindness 'as cost you four pounds fifteen, and that's a curious thing when you come to think of it. Very curious."

"Wot d'ye mean?" I ses.

"Why," he ses, grinning like a madman, "it's just wot we lost between us. I lost a watch and chain worth two pounds, and another couple o' pounds besides; Joe lost ten shillings over 'is di'mond ring; and Charlie lost five bob over a pipe. That's four pounds fifteen—just the same as you."

Them silly fools stood there choking and sobbing and patting each other on the back as though they'd never leave off, and all of a sudden I 'ad a 'orrible suspicion that I 'ad been done.

"Did you see the sovereigns in the box?" I ses, turning to the skipper.

"No," he ses, shaking his 'ead.

Paying Off

" 'Ow do you know they was there, then?"
ses I.

"Because you took charge of 'em," said the
skipper; "and I know wot a clever, sharp chap
you are. It stands to reason that you wouldn't
be responsible for a box like that unless you saw
inside of it. Why, a child o' five wouldn't!"

I stood there looking at 'im, but he couldn't
meet my eye. None of 'em could; and arter
waiting there for a minute or two to give 'em a
chance, I turned my back on 'em and went off to
my dooty.

Made to Measure

Made to Measure

MR. MOTT brought his niece home from
the station with considerable pride.
Although he had received a photograph to
assist identification, he had been very dubious
about accosting the pretty, well-dressed girl who
had stepped from the train and gazed around
with dove-like eyes in search of him. Now he
was comfortably conscious of the admiring gaze
of his younger fellow-townsmen.

"You'll find it a bit dull after London, I
expect," he remarked, as he inserted his key in
the door of a small house in a quiet street.

"I'm tired of London," said Miss Garland.
"I think this is a beautiful little old town—so
peaceful."

Mr. Mott looked gratified.

"I hope you'll stay a long time," he said,

as he led the way into the small front room. "I'm a lonely old man."

His niece sank into an easy chair, and looked about her.

"Thank you," she said, slowly. "I hope I shall. I feel better already. There is so much to upset one in London."

"Noise?" queried Mr. Mott.

"And other things," said Miss Garland, with a slight shudder.

Mr. Mott sighed in sympathy with the unknown, and, judging by his niece's expression, the unknowable. He rearranged the teacups, and, going to the kitchen, returned in a few minutes with a pot of tea.

"Mrs. Pett leaves at three," he said, in explanation, "to look after her children, but she comes back again at eight to look after my supper. And how is your mother?"

Miss Garland told him.

"Last letter I had from her," said Mr. Mott, stealing a glance at the girl's ring-finger, "I understood you were engaged."

Made to Measure

His niece drew herself up.

"Certainly not," she said, with considerable vigour. "I have seen too much of married life. I prefer my freedom. Besides, I don't like men."

Mr. Mott said modestly that he didn't wonder at it, and, finding the subject uncongenial, turned the conversation on to worthier subjects. Miss Garland's taste, it seemed, lay in the direction of hospital nursing, or some other occupation beneficial to mankind at large. Simple and demure, she filled the simpler Mr. Mott with a strong sense of the shortcomings of his unworthy sex.

Within two days, under the darkling glance of Mrs. Pett, she had altered the arrangements of the house. Flowers appeared on the meal-table, knives and forks were properly cleaned, and plates no longer appeared ornamented with the mustard of a previous meal. Fresh air circulated through the house, and, passing from Mrs. Pett's left knee to the lumbar region of Mr. Mott, went on its beneficent way rejoicing.

Made to Measure

On the fifth day of her visit, Mr. Mott sat alone in the front parlour. The window was closed, the door was closed, and Mr. Mott, sitting in an easy chair with his feet up, was aroused from a sound nap by the door opening to admit a young man, who, deserted by Mrs. Pett, stood bowing awkwardly in the doorway.

"Is Miss Garland in?" he stammered.

Mr. Mott rubbed the remnants of sleep from his eyelids.

"She has gone for a walk," he said, slowly.

The young man stood fingering his hat.

"My name is Hurst," he said, with slight emphasis. "Mr. Alfred Hurst."

Mr. Mott, still somewhat confused, murmured that he was glad to hear it.

"I have come from London to see Florrie," continued the intruder. "I suppose she won't be long?"

Mr. Mott thought not, and after a moment's hesitation invited Mr. Hurst to take a chair.

"I suppose she told you we are engaged?" said the latter.

Made to Measure

"Engaged!" said the startled Mr. Mott. "Why, she told me she didn't like men."

"Playfulness," replied Mr. Hurst, with an odd look. "Ah, here she is!"

The handle of the front door turned, and a moment later the door of the room was opened and the charming head of Miss Garland appeared in the opening.

"Back again," she said, brightly. "I've just been——"

She caught sight of Mr. Hurst, and the words died away on her lips. The door slammed, and the two gentlemen, exchanging glances, heard a hurried rush upstairs and the slamming of another door. Also a key was heard to turn sharply in a lock.

"She doesn't want to see you," said Mr. Mott, staring.

The young man turned pale.

"Perhaps she has gone upstairs to take her things off," he muttered, resuming his seat. "Don't—don't hurry her!"

"I wasn't going to," said Mr. Mott.

Made to Measure

He twisted his beard uneasily, and at the end of ten minutes looked from the clock to Mr. Hurst and coughed.

"If you wouldn't mind letting her know I'm waiting," said the young man, brokenly.

Mr. Mott rose, and went slowly upstairs. More slowly still, after an interval of a few minutes, he came back again.

"She doesn't want to see you," he said, slowly.

Mr. Hurst gasped.

"I—I must see her," he faltered.

"She won't see you," repeated Mr. Mott. "And she told me to say she was surprised at you following her down here."

Mr. Hurst uttered a faint moan, and with bent head passed into the little passage and out into the street, leaving Mr. Mott to return to the sitting-room and listen to such explanations as Miss Garland deemed advisable. Great goodness of heart in the face of persistent and unwelcome attentions appeared to be responsible for the late engagement.

Made to Measure

"Well, it's over now," said her uncle, kindly, "and no doubt he'll soon find somebody else. There are plenty of girls would jump at him, I expect."

Miss Garland shook her head.

"He said he couldn't live without me," she remarked, soberly.

Mr. Mott laughed.

"In less than three months I expect he'll be congratulating himself," he said, cheerfully. "Why, I was nearly cau—married, four times. It's a silly age."

His niece said "Indeed!" and, informing him in somewhat hostile tones that she was suffering from a severe headache, retired to her room.

Mr. Mott spent the evening by himself, and retiring to bed at ten-thirty was awakened by a persistent knocking at the front door at half-past one. Half awakened, he lit a candle, and, stumbling downstairs, drew back the bolt of the door, and stood gaping angrily at the pathetic features of Mr. Hurst.

"Sorry to disturb you," said the young man,

59

"but would you mind giving this letter to Miss Garland?"

"Sorry to disturb me!" stuttered Mr. Mott. "What do you mean by it? Eh? What do you mean by it?"

"It is important," said Mr. Hurst. "I can't rest. I've eaten nothing all day."

"Glad to hear it," snapped the irritated Mr. Mott.

"If you will give her that letter, I shall feel easier," said Mr. Hurst.

"I'll give it to her in the morning," said the other, snatching it from him. "Now get off."

Mr. Hurst still murmuring apologies, went, and Mr. Mott, also murmuring, returned to bed. The night was chilly, and it was some time before he could get to sleep again. He succeeded at last, only to be awakened an hour later by a knocking more violent than before. In a state of mind bordering upon frenzy, he dived into his trousers again and went blundering downstairs in the dark.

"Sorry to——" began Mr. Hurst.

Made to Measure

Mr. Mott made uncouth noises at him.

"I have altered my mind," said the young man. "Would you mind letting me have that letter back again? It was too final."

"You—get—off!" said the other, trembling with cold and passion.

"I must have that letter," said Mr. Hurst, doggedly. "All my future happiness may depend upon it."

Mr. Mott, afraid to trust himself with speech, dashed upstairs, and after a search for the matches found the letter, and, returning to the front door, shut it on the visitor's thanks. His niece's door opened as he passed it, and a gentle voice asked for enlightenment.

"How silly of him!" she said, softly. "I hope he won't catch cold. *What* did you say?"

"I was coughing," said Mr. Mott, hastily.

"You'll get cold if you're not careful," said his thoughtful niece. "That's the worst of men, they never seem to have any thought. Did he seem angry, or mournful, or what? I suppose you couldn't see his face?"

Made to Measure

"I didn't try," said Mr. Mott, crisply. "Good night."

By the morning his ill-humour had vanished, and he even became slightly facetious over the events of the night. The mood passed at the same moment that Mr. Hurst passed the window.

"Better have him in and get it over," he said, irritably.

Miss Garland shuddered.

"Never!" she said, firmly. "He'd be down on his knees. It would be too painful. You don't know him."

"Don't want to," said Mr. Mott.

He finished his breakfast in silence, and, after a digestive pipe, proposed a walk. The profile of Mr. Hurst, as it went forlornly past the window again, served to illustrate Miss Garland's refusal.

"I'll go out and see him," said Mr. Mott, starting up. "Are you going to be a prisoner here until this young idiot chooses to go home? It's preposterous!"

Made to Measure

He crammed his hat on firmly and set out in pursuit of Mr. Hurst, who was walking slowly up the street, glancing over his shoulder.

"Morning!" said Mr. Mott, fiercely.

"Good morning," said the other.

"Now, look here," said Mr. Mott. "This has gone far enough, and I won't have any more of it. Why, you ought to be ashamed of yourself, chivvying a young lady that doesn't want you. Haven't you got any pride?"

"No," said the young man, "not where she is concerned."

"I don't believe you have," said the other, regarding him, "and I expect that's where the trouble is. Did she ever have reason to think you were looking after any other girls?"

"Never, I swear it," said Mr. Hurst, eagerly.

"Just so," said Mr. Mott, with a satisfied nod. "That's where you made a mistake. She was too sure of you; it was too easy. No excitement. Girls like a man that other girls want; they don't want a turtle-dove in fancy trousers."

Made to Measure

Mr. Hurst coughed.

"And they like a determined man," continued Miss Garland's uncle. "Why, in my young days, if I had been jilted, and come down to see about it, d'you think I'd have gone out of the house without seeing her? I might have been put out—by half-a-dozen—but I'd have taken the mantelpiece and a few other things with me. And you are bigger than I am."

"We aren't all made the same," said Mr. Hurst, feebly.

"No, we're not," said Mr. Mott. "I'm not blaming you; in a way, I'm sorry for you. If you're not born with a high spirit, nothing'll give it to you."

"It might be learnt," said Mr. Hurst.

Mr. Mott laughed.

"High spirits are born, not made," he said. "The best thing you can do is to go and find another girl, and marry her before she finds you out."

Mr. Hurst shook his head.

"There's no other girl for me," he said, mis-

Made to Measure

erably. "And everything seemed to be going so well. We've been buying things for the house for the last six months, and I've just got a good rise in my screw."

"It'll do for another girl," said Mr. Mott, briskly. "Now, you get off back to town. You are worrying Florrie by staying here, and you are doing no good to anybody. Good-bye."

"I'll walk back as far as the door with you," said Mr. Hurst. "You've done me good. It's a pity I didn't meet you before."

Mr. Mott smiled.

"Remember what I've told you, and you'll do well yet," he said, patting the young man on the arm.

"I will," said Mr. Hurst, and walked on by his side, deep in thought.

"I can't ask you in," said Mr. Mott, jocularly, as he reached his door, and turned the key in the lock. "Good-bye."

"Good-bye," said Mr. Hurst.

He grasped the other's outstretched hand, and with a violent jerk pulled him into the street. Then he pushed open the door, and, slipping into the passage, passed hastily into the front room, closely followed by the infuriated Mr. Mott.

"What — what — what!" stammered that gentleman.

"I'm taking your tip," said Mr. Hurst, pale but determined. "I'm going to stay here until I have seen Florrie."

"You—you're a serpent," said Mr. Mott, struggling for breath. "I—I'm surprised at you. You go out before you get hurt."

"Not without the mantelpiece," said Mr. Hurst, with a distorted grin.

"A viper!" said Mr. Mott, with extreme bitterness. "If you are not out in two minutes I'll send for the police."

"Florrie wouldn't like that," said Mr. Hurst. "She's awfully particular about what people think. You just trot upstairs and tell her that a gentleman wants to see her."

He threw himself into Mr. Mott's own particular easy chair, and, crossing his knees, turned

a deaf ear to the threats of that incensed gentleman. Not until the latter had left the room
did his features reveal the timorousness of the
soul within. Muffled voices sounded from upstairs, and it was evident that an argument of
considerable length was in progress. It was
also evident from the return of Mr. Mott alone
that his niece had had the best of it.

"I've done all I could," he said, "but she de-
clines to see you. She says she won't see you
if you stay here for a month, and you couldn't
do that, you know."

"Why not?" inquired Mr. Hurst.

"Why not?" repeated Mr. Mott, repressing
his feelings with some difficulty. *"Food!"*

Mr. Hurst started.

"And drink," said Mr. Mott, following up
his advantage. "There's no good in starving
yourself for nothing, so you may as well
go."

"When I've seen Florrie," said the young
man, firmly.

Mr. Mott slammed the door, and for the

Made to Measure

rest of the day Mr. Hurst saw him no more. At one o'clock a savoury smell passed the door on its way upstairs, and at five o'clock a middle-aged woman with an inane smile looked into the room on her way aloft with a loaded tea-tray. By supper-time he was suffering considerably from hunger and thirst.

At ten o'clock he heard the footsteps of Mr. Mott descending the stairs. The door opened an inch, and a gruff voice demanded to know whether he was going to stay there all night. Receiving a cheerful reply in the affirmative, Mr. Mott secured the front door with considerable violence, and went off to bed without another word.

He was awakened an hour or two later by the sound of something falling, and, sitting up in bed to listen, became aware of a warm and agreeable odour. It was somewhere about the hour of midnight, but a breakfast smell of eggs and bacon would not be denied.

He put on some clothes and went downstairs. A crack of light showed under the kitchen door,

Made to Measure

and, pushing it open with some force, he gazed spellbound at the spectacle before him.

"Come in," said Mr. Hurst, heartily. "I've just finished."

He rocked an empty beer-bottle and patted another that was half full. Satiety was written on his face as he pushed an empty plate from him, and, leaning back in his chair, smiled lazily at Mr. Mott.

"Go on," said that gentleman, hoarsely.

Mr. Hurst shook his head.

"Enough is as good as a feast," he said, reasonably. "I'll have some more to-morrow."

"Oh, will you?" said the other. "Will you?"

Mr. Hurst nodded, and, opening his coat, disclosed a bottle of beer in each breast-pocket. The other pockets, it appeared, contained food.

"And here's the money for it," he said, putting down some silver on the table. "I am determined, but honest."

With a sweep of his hand, Mr. Mott sent the money flying.

Made to Measure

"To-morrow morning I send for the police. Mind that!" he roared.

"I'd better have my breakfast early, then," said Mr. Hurst, tapping his pockets. "Good night. And thank you for your advice."

He sat for some time after the disappearance of his host, and then, returning to the front room, placed a chair at the end of the sofa and, with the tablecloth for a quilt, managed to secure a few hours' troubled sleep. At eight o'clock he washed at the scullery sink, and at ten o'clock Mr. Mott, with an air of great determination, came in to deliver his ultimatum.

"If you're not outside the front door in five minutes, I'm going to fetch the police," he said, fiercely.

"I want to see Florrie," said the other.

"Well, you won't see her," shouted Mr. Mott.

Mr. Hurst stood feeling his chin.

"Well, would you mind taking a message for me?" he asked. "I just want you to ask her

Made to Measure

whether I am really free. Ask her whether I am free to marry again."

Mr. Mott eyed him in amazement.

"You see, I only heard from her mother," pursued Mr. Hurst, "and a friend of mine who is in a solicitor's office says that isn't good enough. I only came down here to make sure, and I think the least she can do is to tell me herself. If she won't see me, perhaps she'd put it in writing. You see, there's another lady."

"But——" said the mystified Mr. Mott. "You told me——"

"You tell her that," said the other.

Mr. Mott stood for a few seconds staring at him, and then without a word turned on his heel and went upstairs. Left to himself, Mr. Hurst walked nervously up and down the room, and, catching sight of his face in the old-fashioned glass on the mantel-piece, heightened its colour by a few pinches. The minutes seemed interminable, but at last he heard the steps of Mr. Mott on the stairs again.

Made to Measure

"She's coming down to see you herself," said the latter, solemnly.

Mr. Hurst nodded, and, turning to the window, tried in vain to take an interest in passing events. A light step sounded on the stairs, the door creaked, and he turned to find himself confronted by Miss Garland.

"Uncle told me——" she began, coldly.

Mr. Hurst bowed.

"I am sorry to have caused you so much trouble," he said, trying to control his voice, "but you see my position, don't you?"

"No," said the girl.

"Well, I wanted to make sure," said Mr. Hurst. "It's best for all of us, isn't it? Best for you, best for me, and, of course, for my young lady."

"You never said anything about her before," said Miss Garland, her eyes darkening.

"Of course not," said Mr. Hurst. "How could I? I was engaged to you, and then she wasn't my young lady; but, of course, as soon as you broke it off——"

Made to Measure

"Who is she?" inquired Miss Garland, in a casual voice.

"You don't know her," said Mr. Hurst.

"What is she like?"

"I can't describe her very well," said Mr. Hurst. "I can only say she's the most beautiful girl I have ever seen. I think that's what made me take to her. And she's easily pleased. She liked the things I have been buying for the house tremendously."

"Did she?" said Miss Garland, with a gasp.

"All except that pair of vases you chose," continued the veracious Mr. Hurst. "She says they are in bad taste, but she can give them to the charwoman."

"Oh!" said the girl. "Oh, indeed! Very kind of her. Isn't there anything else she doesn't like?"

Mr. Hurst stood considering.

"She doesn't like the upholstering of the best chairs," he said at last. "She thinks they are too showy, so she's going to put covers over them."

Made to Measure

There was a long pause, during which Mr. Mott, taking his niece gently by the arm, assisted her to a chair.

"Otherwise she is quite satisfied," concluded Mr. Hurst.

Miss Garland took a deep breath, but made no reply.

"I have got to satisfy her that I am free," said the young man, after another pause. "I suppose that I can do so?"

"I—I'll think it over," said Miss Garland, in a low voice. "I am not sure what is the right thing to do. I don't want to see you made miserable for life. It's nothing to me, of course, but still——"

She got up and, shaking off the proffered assistance of her uncle, went slowly and languidly up to her room. Mr. Mott followed her as far as the door, and then turned indignantly upon Mr. Hurst.

"You—you've broke her heart," he said, solemnly.

"That's all right," said Mr. Hurst, with a delighted wink. "I'll mend it again."

74

Sam's Ghost

Sam's Ghost

YES, I know, said the night-watchman, thoughtfully, as he sat with a cold pipe in his mouth gazing across the river. I've 'eard it afore. People tell me they don't believe in ghosts and make a laugh of 'em, and all I say is: let them take on a night-watchman's job. Let 'em sit 'ere all alone of a night with the water lapping against the posts and the wind moaning in the corners; especially if a pal of theirs has slipped overboard, and there is little nasty bills stuck up just outside in the High Street offering a reward for the body. Twice men 'ave fallen overboard from this jetty, and I've 'ad to stand my watch here the same night, and not a farthing more for it.

One of the worst and artfullest ghosts I ever 'ad anything to do with was Sam Bullet. He was a waterman at the stairs near by 'ere; the sort o' man that 'ud get you to pay for drinks, and drink yours up by mistake arter he 'ad finished his own. The sort of man that 'ad always left his baccy-box at 'ome, but always 'ad a big pipe in 'is pocket.

He fell overboard off of a lighter one evening, and all that his mates could save was 'is cap. It was on'y two nights afore that he 'ad knocked down an old man and bit a policeman's little finger to the bone, so that, as they pointed out to the widder, p'r'aps he was taken for a wise purpose. P'r'aps he was 'appier where he was than doing six months.

"He was the sort o' chap that'll make himself 'appy *anywhere*," ses one of 'em, comforting-like.

"Not without me," ses Mrs. Bullet, sobbing, and wiping her eyes on something she used for a pocket-hankercher. "He never could bear to be away from me. Was there no last words?"

"On'y one," ses one o' the chaps, Joe Peel by name.

"As 'e fell overboard," ses the other.

78

Sam's Ghost

Mrs. Bullet began to cry agin, and say wot a good 'usband he 'ad been. "Seventeen years come Michaelmas," she ses, "and never a cross word. Nothing was too good for me. Nothing. I 'ad only to ask to 'ave."

"Well, he's gorn now," ses Joe, "and we thought we ought to come round and tell you."

"So as you can tell the police," ses the other chap.

That was 'ow I came to hear of it fust; a policeman told me that night as I stood outside the gate 'aving a quiet pipe. *He* wasn't shedding tears; his only idea was that Sam 'ad got off too easy.

"Well, well," I ses, trying to pacify 'im, "he won't bite no more fingers; there's no policemen where he's gorn to."

He went off grumbling and telling me to be careful, and I put my pipe out and walked up and down the wharf thinking. On'y a month afore I 'ad lent Sam fifteen shillings on a gold watch and chain wot he said an uncle 'ad left 'im. I wasn't wearing it because 'e said 'is

Sam's Ghost

uncle wouldn't like it, but I 'ad it in my pocket, and I took it out under one of the lamps and wondered wot I ought to do.

My fust idea was to take it to Mrs. Bullet, and then, all of a sudden, the thought struck me: *"Suppose he 'adn't come by it honest?"*

I walked up and down agin, thinking. If he 'adn't, and it was found out, it would blacken his good name and break 'is pore wife's 'art. That's the way I looked at it, and for his sake and 'er sake I determined to stick to it.

I felt 'appier in my mind when I 'ad decided on that, and I went round to the Bear's Head and 'ad a pint. Arter that I 'ad another, and then I come back to the wharf and put the watch and chain on and went on with my work.

Every time I looked down at the chain on my waistcoat it reminded me of Sam. I looked on to the river and thought of 'im going down on the ebb. Then I got a sort o' lonesome feeling standing on the end of the jetty all alone, and I went back to the Bear's Head and 'ad another pint.

Sam's Ghost

They didn't find the body, and I was a'most forgetting about Sam when one evening, as I was sitting on a box waiting to get my breath back to 'ave another go at sweeping, Joe Peel, Sam's mate, came on to the wharf to see me.

He came in a mysterious sort o' way that I didn't like: looking be'ind 'im as though he was afraid of being follered, and speaking in a whisper as if 'e was afraid of being heard. He wasn't a man I liked, and I was glad that the watch and chain was stowed safe away in my trowsis-pocket.

"I've 'ad a shock, watchman," he ses.

"Oh!" I ses.

"A shock wot's shook me all up," he ses, working up a shiver. "I've seen something wot I thought people never could see, and wot I never want to see agin. *I've seen Sam!*"

I thought a bit afore I spoke. "Why, I thought he was drownded," I ses.

" So 'e is," ses Joe. "When I say I've seen 'im I mean that I 'ave seen his *ghost!*"

He began to shiver agin, all over.

Sam's Ghost

"Wot was it like?" I ses, very calm.

"Like Sam," he ses, rather short.

"When was it?" I ses.

"Last night at a quarter to twelve," he ses. "It was standing at my front door waiting for me."

"And 'ave you been shivering like that ever since?" I ses.

"Worse than that," ses Joe, looking at me very 'ard. "It's wearing off now. The ghost gave me a message for you."

I put my 'and in my trowsis-pocket and looked at 'im. Then I walked very slow, towards the gate.

"It gave me a message for you," ses Joe, walking beside me. " 'We was always pals, Joe,' " it ses, " 'you and me, and I want you to pay up fifteen bob for me wot I borrowed off of Bill the watchman. I can't rest until it's paid,' it ses. So here's the fifteen bob, watchman."

He put his 'and in 'is pocket and takes out fifteen bob and 'olds it out to me.

"No, no," I ses. "I can't take your money,

Sam's Ghost

Joe Peel. It wouldn't be right. Pore Sam is welcome to the fifteen bob—I don't want it."

"You must take it," ses Joe. "The ghost said if you didn't it would come to me agin and agin till you did, and I can't stand any more of it."

"I can't 'elp your troubles," I ses.

"You must," ses Joe. " 'Give Bill the fifteen bob,' it ses, 'and he'll give you a gold watch and chain wot I gave 'im to mind till it was paid.' "

I see his little game then. "Gold watch and chain," I ses, laughing. "You must ha' misunderstood it, Joe."

"I understood it right enough," ses Joe, getting a bit closer to me as I stepped outside the gate. "Here's your fifteen bob; are you going to give me that watch and chain?"

"Sartainly not," I ses. "I don't know wot you mean by a watch and chain. *If* I 'ad it and I gave it to anybody, I should give it to Sam's widder, not to you."

Sam's Ghost

"It's nothing to do with 'er," ses Joe, very quick. "Sam was most pertikler about that."

"I expect you dreamt it all," I ses. "Where would pore Sam get a gold watch and chain from? And why should 'e go to you about it? Why didn't 'e come to me? If 'e thinks I 'ave got it let 'im come to me."

"All right, I'll go to the police-station," ses Joe.

"I'll come with you," I ses. "But 'ere's a policeman coming along. Let's go to 'im."

I moved towards 'im, but Joe hung back, and, arter using one or two words that would ha' made any ghost ashamed to know 'im, he sheered off. I 'ad a word or two with the policeman about the weather, and then I went inside and locked the gate.

My idea was that Sam 'ad told Joe about the watch and chain afore he fell overboard. Joe was a nasty customer, and I could see that I should 'ave to be a bit careful. Some men might ha' told the police about it—but I never cared much for them. They're like kids in a

Sam's Ghost

way, always asking questions—most of which you can't answer.

It was a little bit creepy all alone on the wharf that night. I don't deny it. Twice I thought I 'eard something coming up on tiptoe behind me. The second time I was so nervous that I began to sing to keep my spirits up, and I went on singing till three of the hands of the *Susan Emily*, wot was lying alongside, came up from the fo'c'sle and offered to fight me. I was thankful when daylight came.

Five nights arterwards I 'ad the shock of my life. It was the fust night for some time that there was no craft up. A dark night, and a nasty moaning sort of a wind. I 'ad just lighted the lamp at the corner of the warehouse, wot 'ad blown out, and was sitting down to rest afore putting the ladder away, when I 'appened to look along the jetty and saw a head coming up over the edge of it. In the light of the lamp I saw the dead white face of Sam Bullet's ghost making faces at me.

I just caught my breath, sharp like, and then

turned and ran for the gate like a race-horse.
I 'ad left the key in the padlock, in case of anything happening, and I just gave it one turn,
flung the wicket open and slammed it in the
ghost's face, and tumbled out into the road.

I ran slap into the arms of a young policeman
wot was passing. Nasty, short-tempered chap
he was, but I don't think I was more glad to see
anybody in my life. I hugged 'im till 'e nearly
lost 'is breath, and then he sat me down on the
kerb-stone and asked me wot I meant by it.

Wot with the excitement and the running I
couldn't speak at fust, and when I did he said
I was trying to deceive 'im.

"There ain't no such thing as ghosts," he
ses; "you've been drinking."

"It came up out o' the river and run arter me
like the wind," I ses.

"Why didn't it catch you, then?" he ses,
looking me up and down and all round about.
"Talk sense."

He went up to the gate and peeped in, and,
arter watching a moment, stepped inside and

Sam's Ghost

walked down the wharf, with me follering. It was my dooty; besides, I didn't like being left all alone by myself.

Twice we walked up and down and all over the wharf. He flashed his lantern into all the dark corners, into empty barrels and boxes, and then he turned and flashed it right into my face and shook his 'ead at me.

"You've been having a bit of a lark with me," he ses, "and for two pins I'd take you. Mind, if you say a word about this to anybody, I will."

He stalked off with his 'ead in the air, and left me all alone in charge of a wharf with a ghost on it. I stayed outside in the street, of course, but every now and then I fancied I heard something moving about the other side of the gate, and once it was so distinct that I run along to the Bear's Head and knocked 'em up and asked them for a little brandy, for illness.

I didn't get it, of course; I didn't expect to; but I 'ad a little conversation with the landlord from 'is bedroom-winder that did me more good than the brandy would ha' done. Once

or twice I thought he would 'ave fallen out, and
many a man has 'ad his licence taken away for
less than a quarter of wot 'e said to me that
night. Arter he thought he 'ad finished and
was going back to bed agin, I pointed out to 'im
that he 'adn't kissed me "good night," and if it
'adn't ha' been for 'is missis and two grown-up
daughters and the potman I believe he'd ha'
talked to me till daylight.

'Ow I got through the rest of the night I
don't know. It seemed to be twenty nights instead of one, but the day came at last, and when
the hands came on at six o'clock they found the
gate open and me on dooty same as usual.

I slept like a tired child when I got 'ome, and
arter a steak and onions for dinner I sat down
and lit my pipe and tried to think wot was to be
done. One thing I was quite certain about: I
wasn't going to spend another night on that
wharf alone.

I went out arter a bit, as far as the Claren-
don Arms, for a breath of fresh air, and I 'ad
just finished a pint and was wondering whether

Sam's Ghost

I ought to 'ave another, when Ted Dennis came in, and my mind was made up. He 'ad been in the Army all 'is life, and, so far, he 'ad never seen anything that 'ad frightened 'im. I've seen him myself take on men twice 'is size just for the love of the thing, and, arter knocking them silly, stand 'em a pint out of 'is own pocket. When I asked 'im whether he was afraid of ghosts he laughed so 'ard that the landlord came from the other end of the bar to see wot was the matter.

I stood Ted a pint, and arter he 'ad finished it I told 'im just how things was. I didn't say anything about the watch and chain, because there was no need to, and when we came outside agin I 'ad engaged an assistant-watchman for ninepence a night.

"All you've got to do," I ses, "is to keep me company. You needn't turn up till eight o'clock of a night, and you can leave 'arf an hour afore me in the morning."

"Right-o!" ses Ted. "And if I see the ghost I'll make it wish it 'ad never been born."

Sam's Ghost

It was a load off my mind, and I went 'ome and ate a tea that made my missis talk about the work'ouse, and orstritches in 'uman shape wot would eat a woman out of 'ouse and 'ome if she would let 'em.

I got to the wharf just as it was striking six, and at a quarter to seven the wicket was pushed open gentle and the ugly 'ead of Mr. Joe Peel was shoved inside.

"Hullo!" I ses. "Wot do you want?"

"I want to save your life," he ses, in a solemn voice. "You was within a inch of death last night, watchman."

"Oh!" I ses, careless-like. " 'Ow do you know!"

"The ghost o' Sam Bullet told me," ses Joe. "Arter it 'ad chased you up the wharf screaming for 'elp, it came round and told me all about it."

"It seems fond of you," I ses. "I wonder why?"

"It was in a terrible temper," ses Joe, "and its face was awful to look at. 'Tell the watchman,' it ses, 'that if he don't give you the watch and chain I shall appear to 'im agin and kill 'im.' "

"All right," I ses, looking behind me to where three of the 'ands of the *Daisy* was sitting on the fo'c'sle smoking. "I've got plenty of company to-night."

"Company won't save you," ses Joe. "For the last time, are you going to give me that watch and chain, or not? Here's your fifteen bob."

"No," I ses; "even if I 'ad got it I shouldn't give it to you; and it's no use giving it to the ghost, because, being made of air, he 'asn't got anywhere to put it."

"Very good," ses Joe, giving me a black look. "I've done all I can to save you, but if you won't listen to sense, you won't. You'll see Sam Bullet agin, and you'll not on'y lose the watch and chain but your life as well."

"All right," I ses, "and thank you kindly, but I've got an assistant, as it 'appens—a man wot wants to see a ghost."

Sam's Ghost

"An' assistant?" ses Joe, staring.

"An old soldier," I ses. "A man wot likes trouble and danger. His idea is to shoot the ghost and see wot 'appens."

"*Shoot!*" ses Joe. "Shoot a pore 'armless ghost. Does he want to be 'ung? Ain't it enough for a pore man to be drownded, but wot you must try and shoot 'im arterwards? Why, you ought to be ashamed o' yourself. Where's your 'art?"

"It won't be shot if it don't come on my wharf," I ses. "Though I don't mind if it does when I've got somebody with me. I ain't afraid of anything living, and I don't mind ghosts when there's two of us. Besides which, the noise of the pistol 'll wake up 'arf the river."

"You take care *you* don't get woke up," ses Joe, 'ardly able to speak for temper.

He went off stamping, and grinding 'is teeth, and at eight o'clock to the minute, Ted Dennis turned up with 'is pistol and helped me take care of the wharf. Happy as a skylark 'e was,

Sam's Ghost

and to see him 'iding behind a barrel with his pistol ready, waiting for the ghost, a'most made me forget the expense of it all.

It never came near us that night, and Ted was a bit disappointed next morning as he took 'is ninepence and went off. Next night was the same, and the next, and then Ted gave up hiding on the wharf for it, and sat and snoozed in the office instead.

A week went by, and then another, and still there was no sign of Sam Bullet's ghost, or Joe Peel, and every morning I 'ad to try and work up a smile as I shelled out ninepence for Ted. It nearly ruined me, and, worse than that, I couldn't explain why I was short to the missis. Fust of all she asked me *wot* I was spending it on, then she asked me *who* I was spending it on. It nearly broke up my 'ome— she did smash one kitchen-chair and a vase off the parlour mantelpiece—but I wouldn't tell 'er, and then, led away by some men on strike at Smith's wharf, Ted went on strike for a bob a night.

Sam's Ghost

That was arter he 'ad been with me for three weeks, and when Saturday came, of course I was more short than ever, and people came and stood at their doors all the way down our street to listen to the missis taking my character away.

I stood it as long as I could, and then, when 'er back was turned for 'arf a moment, I slipped out. While she'd been talking I'd been thinking, and it came to me clear as daylight that there was no need for me to sacrifice myself any longer looking arter a dead man's watch and chain.

I didn't know exactly where Joe Peel lived, but I knew the part, and arter peeping into seven public-'ouses I see the man I wanted sitting by 'imself in a little bar. I walked in quiet-like, and sat down opposite 'im.

"Morning," I ses.

Joe Peel grunted.

"'Ave one with me?" I ses.

He grunted agin, but not quite so fierce, and I fetched the two pints from the counter and took a seat alongside of 'im.

Sam's Ghost

"I've been looking for you," I ses.

"Oh!" he ses, looking me up and down and all over. "Well, you've found me now."

"I want to talk to you about the ghost of pore Sam Bullet," I ses.

Joe Peel put 'is mug down sudden and looked at me fierce. "Look 'ere! Don't you come and try to be funny with me," he ses. " 'Cos I won't 'ave it."

"I don't want to be funny," I ses. "Wot I want to know is, are you in the same mind about that watch and chain as you was the other day?"

He didn't seem to be able to speak at fust, but arter a time 'e gives a gasp. "Wot's the game?" he ses.

"Wot I want to know is, if I give you that watch and chain for fifteen bob, will that keep the ghost from 'anging round my wharf agin?" I ses.

"Why, o' course," he ses, staring; "but you ain't been seeing it agin, 'ave you?"

"I've not, and I don't want to," I ses. "If

Sam's Ghost

it wants you to 'ave the watch and chain, give
me the fifteen bob, and it's yours."

He looked at me for a moment as if he
couldn't believe 'is eyesight, and then 'e puts
his 'and into 'is trowsis-pocket and pulls out
one shilling and fourpence, 'arf a clay-pipe, and
a bit o' lead-pencil.

"That's all I've got with me," he ses. "I'll
owe you the rest. You ought to ha' took the
fifteen bob when I 'ad it."

There was no 'elp for it, and arter making
'im swear to give me the rest o' the money
when 'e got it, and that I shouldn't see the
ghost agin, J 'anded the things over to 'im and
came away. He came to the door to see me
off, and if ever a man looked puzzled, 'e did.
Pleased at the same time.

It was a load off of my mind. My conscience told me I'd done right, and arter sending a little boy with a note to Ted Dennis to
tell 'im not to come any more, I felt 'appier
than I 'ad done for a long time. When I got
to the wharf that evening it seemed like a

Sam's Ghost

diff'rent place, and I was whistling and smiling over my work quite in my old way, when the young policeman passed.

"Hullo!" he ses. " 'Ave you seen the ghost agin?"

"I 'ave not," I ses, drawing myself up. " 'Ave you?"

"No," he ses. "We missed it."

"Missed it?" I ses, staring at 'im.

"Yes," he ses, nodding. "The day arter you came out screaming, and cuddling me like a frightened baby, it shipped as A.B. on the barque *Ocean King*, for Valparaiso. We missed it by a few hours. Next time you see a ghost, knock it down fust and go and cuddle the police arterwards."

Bedridden

Bedridden

July 12, 1915.—Disquieting rumours to the effect that epidemic of Billetitis hitherto confined to the north of King's Road shows signs of spreading.

July 14.—Report that two Inns of Court men have been seen peeping over my gate.

July 16.—Informed that soldier of agreeable appearance and charming manners requests interview with me. Took a dose of Phospherine and went. Found composite photograph of French, Joffre, and Hindenburg waiting for me in the hall. Smiled (he did, I mean) and gave me the mutilated form of salute reserved for civilians. Introduced himself as Quartermaster-Sergeant Beddem, and stated that the Inns of Court O.T.C. was going under canvas next week. After which he gulped. Meantime could I take in *a* billet.

Bedridden

Questioned as to what day the corps was going into camp said that he believed it was Monday, but was not quite sure—might possibly be Tuesday. Swallowed again and coughed a little. Accepted billet and felt completely rewarded by smile. Q.M.S. bade me good-bye, and then with the air of a man suddenly remembering something, asked me whether I could take two. Excused myself and interviewed my C.O. behind the dining-room door. Came back and accepted. Q.M.S. so overjoyed (apparently) that he fell over the scraper. Seemed to jog his memory. He paused, and gazing in absent fashion at the topmost rose on the climber in the porch, asked whether I could take three! Added hopefully that the third was only a boy. Excused myself. Heated debate with C.O. Subject: sheets. Returned with me to explain to the Q.M.S. He smiled. C.O. accepted at once, and, returning smile, expressed regret at size and position of bedrooms available. Q.M.S. went off swinging cane jauntily.

Bedridden

July 17.—Billets arrived. Spoke to them about next Monday and canvas. They seemed surprised. Strange how the military authorities decline to take men into their confidence merely because they are privates. Let them upstairs. They went (for first and last time) on tiptoe.

July 18.—Saw Q.M.S. Beddem in the town. Took shelter in the King's Arms.

Aug. 3.—Went to Cornwall.

Aug. 31.—Returned. Billets received me very hospitably.

Sept. 4.—Private Budd, electrical engineer, dissatisfied with appearance of bell-push in dining-room, altered it.

Sept. 5.—Bells out of order.

Sept. 6.—Private Merited, also an electrical engineer, helped Private Budd to repair bells.

Sept. 7.—Private Budd helped Private Merited to repair bells.

Sept. 8.—Privates Budd and Merited helped each other to repair bells.

Bedridden

Sept. 9.—Sent to local tradesman to put my bells in order.

Sept. 15.—Told that Q.M.S. Beddem wished to see me. Saw C.O. first. She thought he had possibly come to take some of the billets away. Q.M.S. met my approach with a smile that reminded me vaguely of picture-postcards I had seen. Awfully sorry to trouble me, but Private Montease, just back from three weeks' holiday with bronchitis, was sleeping in the wood-shed on three planks and a tin-tack. Beamed at me and waited. Went and bought another bedstead.

Sept. 16.—Private Montease and a cough entered into residence.

Sept. 17, 11.45 p.m.—Maid came to bedroom-door with some cough lozenges which she asked me to take to the new billet. Took them. Private Montease thanked me, but said he didn't mind coughing. Said it was an heirloom; Montease cough, known in highest circles all over Scotland since time of Young Pretender.

Bedridden

Sept. 20.—Private Montease installed in easy-chair in dining-room with touch of bronchitis, looking up trains to Bournemouth.

Sept. 21.—Private Montease in bed all day. Cook anxious "to do her bit" rubbed his chest with home-made embrocation. Believe it is same stuff she rubs chests in hall with. Smells the same anyway.

Sept. 24.—Private Montease, complaining of slight rawness of chest, but otherwise well, returned to duty.

Oct. 5.—Cough worse again. Private Montease thinks that with care it may turn to bronchitis. Borrowed an A.B.C.

Oct. 6.—Private Montease relates uncanny experience. Woke up with feeling of suffocation to find an enormous black-currant and glycerine jujube wedged in his gullet. Never owned such a thing in his life. Seems to be unaware that he always sleeps with his mouth open.

Nov. 14.—Private Bowser, youngest and tallest of my billets, gazetted.

Bedridden

Nov. 15, 10.35 *a.m.*—Private Bowser in tip-top spirits said good-bye to us all.

10.45.—Told that Q.M.S. Beddem desired to see me. Capitulated. New billet, Private Early, armed to the teeth, turned up in the evening. Said that he was a Yorkshireman. Said that Yorkshire was the finest county in England, and Yorkshiremen the finest men in the world. Stood toying with his bayonet and waiting for contradiction.

Jan. 5, 1916.—Standing in the garden just after lunch was witness to startling phenomenon. Q.M.S. Beddem came towards front-gate with a smile so expansive that gate after first trembling violently on its hinges swung open of its own accord. Q.M.S., with smile (sad), said he was in trouble. Very old member of the Inns of Court, Private Keen, had rejoined, and he wanted a good billet for him. Would cheerfully give up his own bed, but it wasn't long enough. Not to be outdone in hospitality by my own gate accepted Private Keen. Q.M.S. digging hole in my path with toe of

Bedridden

right boot, and for first and only time manifesting signs of nervousness, murmured that two life-long friends of Private Keen's had rejoined with him. Known as the Three Inseparables. Where they were to sleep, unless I———. Fled to house, and locking myself in top-attic watched Q.M.S. from window. He departed with bent head and swagger-cane reversed.

Jan 6.—Private Keen arrived. Turned out to be son of an old Chief of mine. Resolved not to visit the sins of the father on the head of a child six feet two high and broad in proportion.

Feb. 6.—Private Keen came home with a temperature.

Feb. 7.—M.O. diagnosed influenza. Was afraid it would spread.

Feb. 8.—Warned the other four billets. They seemed amused. Pointed out that influenza had no terrors for men in No. 2 Company, who were doomed to weekly night-ops. under Major Carryon.

Feb. 9.—House strangely and pleasantly

Bedridden

quiet. Went to see how Private Keen was progressing, and found the other four billets sitting in a row on his bed practising deep-breathing exercises.

Feb. 16.—Billets on night-ops. until late hour. Spoke in highest terms of Major Carry-on's marching powers—also in other terms.

March 3.—Waited up until midnight for Private Merited, who had gone to Slough on his motor-bike.

March 4, 1.5 *a.m.*—Awakened by series of explosions from over-worked, or badly-worked, motor-bike. Put head out of window and threw key to Private Merited. He seemed excited. Said he had been chased all the way from Chesham by a pink rat with yellow spots. Advised him to go to bed. Set him an example.

1.10. *a.m.*—Heard somebody in the pantry.

2.10. *a.m.*—Heard Private Merited going upstairs to bed.

2.16 *a.m.*—Heard Private Merited still going upstairs to bed.

Bedridden

2.20-3.15. a.m.—Heard Private Merited *getting* to bed.

April 3, 12.30 a.m.—Town-hooter announced Zeppelins and excited soldier called up my billets from their beds to go and frighten them off. Pleasant to see superiority of billets over the hooter: *that* only emitted three blasts.

12.50 a.m.—Billets returned with exception of Private Merited, who was retained for sake of his motor-bike.

9 a.m.—On way to bath-room ran into Private Merited, who, looking very glum and sleepy, inquired whether I had a copy of the *Exchange and Mart* in the house.

10 p.m.—Overheard billets discussing whether it was worth while removing boots before going to bed until the Zeppelin scare was over. Joined in discussion.

May 2.—Rumours that the Inns of Court were going under canvas. Discredited them.

May 5.—Rumours grow stronger.

May 6.—Billets depressed. Begin to think perhaps there is something in rumours after all.

Bedridden

May 9.—All doubts removed. Tents begin to spring up with the suddenness of mushrooms in fields below Berkhamsted Place.

May 18, LIBERATION DAY.—Bade a facetious good-bye to my billets; response lacking in *bonhomie*.

May 19.—House delightfully quiet. Presented caller of unkempt appearance at back-door with remains of pair of military boots, three empty shaving-stick tins, and a couple of partially bald tooth-brushes.

May 21.—In afternoon went round and looked at camp. Came home smiling, and went to favourite seat in garden to smoke. Discovered Private Early lying on it fast asleep. Went to study. Private Merited at table writing long and well-reasoned letter to his tailor. As he said he could never write properly with anybody else in the room, left him and went to bath-room. Door locked. Peevish but familiar voice, with a Scotch accent, asked me what I wanted; also complained of temperature of water.

Bedridden

May 22.—After comparing notes with neighbours, feel deeply grateful to Q.M.S. Beddem for sending me the best six men in the corps.

July 15.—Feel glad to have been associated, however remotely and humbly, with a corps, the names of whose members appear on the Roll of Honour of every British regiment.

The Convert

The Convert

MR. PURNIP took the arm of the new recruit and hung over him almost tenderly as they walked along; Mr. Billing, with a look of conscious virtue on his jolly face, listened with much satisfaction to his friend's compliments.

"It's such an example," said the latter. "Now we've got you the others will follow like sheep. You will be a bright lamp in the darkness."

"Wot's good enough for me *ought* to be good enough for them," said Mr. Billing, modestly. "They'd better not let me catch——"

"*H'sh! H'sh!*" breathed Mr. Purnip, tilting his hat and wiping his bald, benevolent head.

"I forgot," said the other, with something like a sigh. "No more fighting; but suppose somebody hits me?"

"Turn the other cheek," replied Mr. Purnip.

The Convert

"They won't hit that; and when they see you standing there smiling at them——"

"After being hit?" interrupted Mr. Billing.

"After being hit," assented the other, "they'll be ashamed of themselves, and it'll hurt them more than if you struck them."

"Let's 'ope so," said the convert; "but it don't sound reasonable. I can hit a man pretty 'ard. Not that I'm bad-tempered, mind you; a bit quick, p'r'aps. And, after all, a good smack in the jaw saves any amount of argufying."

Mr. Purnip smiled, and, as they walked along, painted a glowing picture of the influence to be wielded by a first-class fighting-man who refused to fight. It was a rough neighbourhood, and he recognized with sorrow that more respect was paid to a heavy fist than to a noble intellect or a loving heart.

"And you combine them all," he said, patting his companion's arm.

Mr. Billing smiled. "You ought to know best," he said, modestly.

"You'll be surprised to find how easy it is,"

The Convert

continued Mr. Purnip. "You will go from strength to strength. Old habits will disappear, and you will hardly know you have lost them. In a few months' time you will probably be wondering what you could'ever have seen in beer, for example."

"I thought you said you didn't want me to give up beer?" said the other.

"We don't," said Mr. Purnip. "I mean that as you grow in stature you will simply lose the taste for it."

Mr. Billing came to a sudden full stop. "D'ye mean I shall lose my liking for a drop o' beer without being able to help myself?" he demanded, in an anxious voice.

Mr. Purnip coughed.

"Of course, it doesn't happen in every case," he said, hastily.

Mr. Billing's features relaxed. "Well, let's 'ope I shall be one of the fortunate ones," he said, simply. "I can put up with a good deal, but when it comes to beer——"

"We shall see," said the other, smiling.

The Convert

"We don't want to interfere with anybody's comfort; we want to make them happier, that's all. A little more kindness between man and man; a little more consideration for each other; a little more brightness in dull lives."

He paused at the corner of the street, and, with a hearty handshake, went off. Mr. Billing, a prey to somewhat mixed emotions, continued on his way home. The little knot of earnest men and women who had settled in the district to spread light and culture had been angling for him for some time. He wondered, as he walked, what particular bait it was that had done the mischief.

"They've got me at last," he remarked, as he opened the house-door and walked into his small kitchen. "I couldn't say 'no' to Mr. Purnip."

"Wish 'em joy," said Mrs. Billing, briefly. "Did you wipe your boots?"

Her husband turned without a word, and, retreating to the mat, executed a prolonged double-shuffle.

The Convert

"You needn't wear it out," said the surprised Mrs. Billing.

"We've got to make people 'appier," said her husband, seriously; "be kinder to 'em, and brighten up their dull lives a bit. That's wot Mr. Purnip says."

"You'll brighten 'em up all right," declared Mrs. Billing, with a sniff. "I sha'n't forget last Tuesday week—no, not if I live to be a hundred. You'd ha' brightened up the police-station if I 'adn't got you home just in the nick of time."

Her husband, who was by this time busy under the scullery-tap, made no reply. He came from it spluttering, and, seizing a small towel, stood in the door-way burnishing his face and regarding his wife with a smile which Mr. Purnip himself could not have surpassed. He sat down to supper, and between bites explained in some detail the lines on which his future life was to be run. As an earnest of good faith, he consented, after a short struggle, to a slip of oil-cloth for the passage; a pair of vases for the

The Convert

front room; and a new and somewhat expensive corn-cure for Mrs. Billing.

"And let's 'ope you go on as you've begun," said that gratified lady. "There's something in old Purnip after all. I've been worrying you for months for that oilcloth. Are you going to help me wash up? Mr. Purnip would."

Mr. Billing appeared not to hear, and, taking up his cap, strolled slowly in the direction of the Blue Lion. It was a beautiful summer evening, and his bosom swelled as he thought of the improvements that a little brotherliness might effect in Elk Street. Engrossed in such ideas, it almost hurt him to find that, as he entered one door of the Blue Lion, two gentlemen, forgetting all about their beer, disappeared through the other.

"Wot 'ave they run away like that for?" he demanded, looking round. "I wouldn't hurt 'em."

"Depends on wot you call hurting, Joe," said a friend.

Mr. Billing shook his head. "They've no

call to be afraid of me," he said, gravely. "I wouldn't hurt a fly; I've got a new 'art."

"A new wot?" inquired his friend, staring.

"A new 'art," repeated the other. "I've given up fighting and swearing, and drinking too much. I'm going to lead a new life and do all the good I can; I'm going——"

"Glory! Glory!" ejaculated a long, thin youth, and, making a dash for the door, disappeared.

"He'll know me better in time," said Mr. Billing. "Why, I wouldn't hurt a fly. I want to do good to people; not to hurt 'em. I'll have a pint," he added, turning to the bar.

"Not here you won't," said the landlord, eyeing him coldly.

"Why not?" demanded the astonished Mr. Billing.

"You've had all you ought to have already," was the reply. "And there's one thing I'll swear to—you ain't had it 'ere."

"I haven't 'ad a drop pass my lips——" began the outraged Mr. Billing.

The Convert

"Yes, I know," said the other, wearily, as he shifted one or two glasses and wiped the counter; "I've heard it all before, over and over again. Mind you, I've been in this business thirty years, and if I don't know when a man's had his whack, and a drop more, nobody does. You get off 'ome and ask your missis to make you a nice cup o' good strong tea, and then get up to bed and sleep it off."

"I dare say," said Mr. Billing, with cold dignity, as he paused at the door—"I dare say I may give up beer altogether."

He stood outside pondering over the unforeseen difficulties attendant upon his new career, moving a few inches to one side as Mr. Ricketts, a foe of long standing, came towards the public-house, and, halting a yard or two away, eyed him warily.

"Come along," said Mr. Billing, speaking somewhat loudly, for the benefit of the men in the bar; "I sha'n't hurt you; my fighting days are over."

"Yes, I dessay," replied the other, edging away.

The Convert

"It's all right, Bill," said a mutual friend, through the half-open door; "he's got a new 'art."

Mr. Ricketts looked perplexed. " 'Art disease, d'ye mean?" he inquired, hopefully. *"Can't* he fight no more?"

"A new 'art," said Mr. Billing. "It's as strong as ever it was, but it's changed—brother."

"If you call me 'brother' agin I'll give you something for yourself, and chance it," said Mr. Ricketts, ferociously. "I'm a pore man, but I've got my pride."

Mr. Billing, with a smile charged with brotherly love, leaned his left cheek towards him. "Hit it," he said, gently.

"Give it a smack and run, Bill," said the voice of a well-wisher inside.

"There'd be no need for 'im to run," said Mr. Billing. "I wouldn't hit 'im back for anything. I should turn the other cheek."

"Whaffor?" inquired the amazed Mr. Ricketts.

The Convert

"For another swipe," said Mr. Billing, radiantly.

In the fraction of a second he got the first, and reeled back staggering. The onlookers from the bar came out hastily. Mr. Ricketts, somewhat pale, stood his ground.

"You see, I don't hit you," said Mr. Billing, with a ghastly attempt at a smile.

He stood rubbing his cheek gently, and, re-membering Mr. Purnip's statements, slowly, inch by inch, turned the other in the direction of his adversary. The circuit was still incom-plete when Mr. Ricketts, balancing himself carefully, fetched it a smash that nearly burst it. Mr. Billing, somewhat jarred by his con-tact with the pavement, rose painfully and confronted him.

"I've only got two cheeks, mind," he said, slowly.

Mr. Ricketts sighed. "I wish you'd got a blinking dozen," he said, wistfully. "Well, so long. Be good."

He walked into the Blue Lion absolutely

The Convert

free from that sense of shame which Mr. Purnip had predicted, and, accepting a pint from
an admirer, boasted noisily of his exploit. Mr.
Billing, suffering both mentally and physically,
walked slowly home to his astonished wife.

"P'r'aps he'll be ashamed of hisself when 'e
comes to think it over," he murmured, as Mrs.
Billing, rendered almost perfect by practice,
administered first aid.

"I s'pect he's crying his eyes out," she said,
with a sniff. "Tell me if that 'urts."

Mr. Billing told her, then, suddenly remembering himself, issued an expurgated edition.

"I'm sorry for the next man that 'its you,"
said his wife, as she drew back and regarded
her handiwork.

"Well, you needn't be," said Mr. Billing,
with dignity. "It would take more than a
couple o' props in the jaw to make me alter my
mind when I've made it up. You ought to
know that by this time. Hurry up and finish.
I want you to go to the corner and fetch me a
pot."

The Convert

"What, ain't you going out agin?" demanded his astonished wife.

Mr. Billing shook his head. "Somebody else might want to give me one," he said, resignedly, "and I've 'ad about all I want to-night."

His face was still painful next morning, but as he sat at breakfast in the small kitchen he was able to refer to Mr. Ricketts in terms which were an eloquent testimony to Mr. Purnip's teaching. Mrs. Billing, unable to contain herself, wandered off into the front room with a duster.

"Are you nearly ready to go?" she inquired, returning after a short interval.

"Five minutes," said Mr. Billing, nodding. I'll just light my pipe and then I'm off."

" 'Cos there's two or three waiting outside for you," added his wife.

Mr. Billing rose. "Ho, is there?" he said, grimly, as he removed his coat and proceeded to roll up his shirt-sleeves. "I'll learn 'em. I'll give 'em something to wait for. I'll——"

The Convert

His voice died away as he saw the triumph in his wife's face, and, drawing down his sleeves again, he took up his coat and stood eyeing her in genuine perplexity.

"Tell 'em I've gorn," he said, at last.

"And what about telling lies?" demanded his wife. "What would your Mr. Purnip say to that?"

"You do as you're told," exclaimed the harassed Mr. Billing. *"I'm* not going to tell 'em; it's you."

Mrs. Billing returned to the parlour, and, with Mr. Billing lurking in the background, busied herself over a china flower-pot that stood in the window, and turned an anxious eye upon three men waiting outside. After a glance or two she went to the door.

"Did you want to see my husband?" she inquired.

The biggest of the three nodded. "Yus," he said, shortly.

"I'm sorry," said Mrs. Billing, "but he 'ad to go early this morning. Was it anything partikler?"

The Convert

"Gorn?" said the other, in disappointed tones. "Well, you tell 'im I'll see 'im later on."

He turned away, and, followed by the other two, walked slowly up the road. Mr. Billing, after waiting till the coast was clear, went off in the other direction.

He sought counsel of his friend and mentor that afternoon, and stood beaming with pride at the praise lavished upon him. Mr. Purnip's co-workers were no less enthusiastic than their chief; and various suggestions were made to Mr. Billing as to his behaviour in the unlikely event of further attacks upon his noble person.

He tried to remember the suggestions in the harassing days that followed; baiting Joe Billing becoming popular as a pastime from which no evil results need be feared. It was creditable to his fellow-citizens that most of them refrained from violence with a man who declined to hit back, but as a butt his success was assured. The night when a gawky lad of eighteen drank up his beer, and then invited him to step outside

The Convert

if he didn't like it, dwelt long in his memory.
And Elk Street thrilled one evening at the sight
of their erstwhile champion flying up the road
hotly pursued by a foeman half his size. His
explanation to his indignant wife that, having
turned the other cheek the night before, he was
in no mood for further punishment, was received in chilling silence.

"They'll soon get tired of it," he said, hopefully; "and I ain't going to be beat by a lot of
chaps wot I could lick with one 'and tied behind
me. They'll get to understand in time; Mr.
Purnip says so. It's a pity that you don't try
and do some good yourself."

Mrs. Billing received the suggestion with a
sniff; but the seed was sown. She thought the
matter over in private, and came to the conclu-
sion that, if her husband wished her to partici-
pate in good works, it was not for her to deny
him. Hitherto her efforts in that direction
had been promptly suppressed; Mr. Billing's
idea being that if a woman looked after her
home and her husband properly there should be

The Convert

neither time nor desire for anything else. His surprise on arriving home to tea on Saturday afternoon, and finding a couple of hard-working neighbours devouring his substance, almost deprived him of speech.

"Poor things," said his wife, after the guests had gone; "they did enjoy it. It's cheered 'em up wonderful. You and Mr. Purnip are quite right. I can see that now. You can tell him that it was you what put it into my 'art."

"Me? Why, I never dreamt o' such a thing," declared the surprised Mr. Billing. "And there's other ways of doing good besides asking a pack of old women in to tea."

"I know there is," said his wife. "All in good time," she added, with a far-away look in her eyes.

Mr. Billing cleared his throat, but nothing came of it. He cleared it again.

"I couldn't let you do all the good," said his wife, hastily. "It wouldn't be fair. I must help."

Mr. Billing lit his pipe noisily, and then took

The Convert

it out into the back-yard and sat down to think over the situation. The ungenerous idea that his wife was making goodness serve her own ends was the first that occurred to him.

His suspicions increased with time. Mrs. Billing's good works seemed to be almost entirely connected with hospitality. True, she had entertained Mr. Purnip and one of the ladies from the Settlement to tea, but that only riveted his bonds more firmly. Other visitors included his sister-in-law, for whom he had a great distaste, and some of the worst-behaved children in the street.

"It's only high spirits," said Mrs. Billing; "all children are like that. And I do it to help the mothers."

"And 'cos you like children," said her husband, preserving his good-humour with an effort.

There was a touch of monotony about the new life, and the good deeds that accompanied it, which, to a man of ardent temperament, was apt to pall. And Elk Street, instead of giving him the credit which was his due, preferred to ascribe the change in his behaviour to what they called being "a bit barmy on the crumpet."

He came home one evening somewhat dejected, brightening up as he stood in the passage and inhaled the ravishing odours from the kitchen. Mrs. Billing, with a trace of nervousness somewhat unaccountable in view of the excellent quality of the repast provided, poured him out a glass of beer, and passed flattering comment upon his appearance.

"Wot's the game?" he inquired.

"Game?" repeated his wife, in a trembling voice. "Nothing. 'Ow do you find that steak-pudding? I thought of giving you one every Wednesday."

Mr. Billing put down his knife and fork and sat regarding her thoughtfully. Then he pushed back his chair suddenly, and, a picture of consternation and wrath, held up his hand for silence.

"W-w-wot is it?" he demanded. "A cat?"

Mrs. Billing made no reply, and her husband

The Convert

sprang to his feet as a long, thin wailing sounded through the house. A note of temper crept into it and strengthened it.

"*Wot is it?*" demanded Mr. Billing again.

"It's—it's Mrs. Smith's Charlie," stammered his wife.

"In—in *my* bedroom?" exclaimed her husband, in incredulous accents. "Wot's it doing there?"

"I took it for the night," said his wife hurriedly. "Poor thing, what with the others being ill she's 'ad a dreadful time, and she said if I'd take Charlie for a few—for a night, she might be able to get some sleep."

Mr. Billing choked. "And what about my sleep?" he shouted. "Chuck it outside at once. D'ye hear me?"

His words fell on empty air, his wife having already sped upstairs to pacify Master Smith by a rhythmical and monotonous thumping on the back. Also she lifted up a thin and not particularly sweet voice and sang to him. Mr. Billing, finishing his supper in indignant silence, told himself grimly that he was "beginning to have enough of it."

He spent the evening at the Charlton Arms, and, returning late, went slowly and heavily up to bed. In the light of a shaded candle he saw a small, objectionable-looking infant fast asleep on two chairs by the side of the bed.

"*H'sh!*" said his wife, in a thrilling whisper. "He's just gone off."

"D'ye mean I mustn't open my mouth in my own bedroom?" demanded the indignant man, loudly.

"*H'sh!*" said his wife again.

It was too late. Master Smith, opening first one eye and then the other, finished by opening his mouth. The noise was appalling.

"*H'sh! H'sh!*" repeated Mrs. Billing, as her husband began to add to the noise. "Don't wake 'im right up."

"Right up?" repeated the astonished man. "*Right up?* Why, is he doing this in 'is sleep?"

He subsided into silence, and, undressing with stealthy care, crept into bed and lay there,

The Convert

marvelling at his self-control. He was a sound sleeper, but six times at least he was awakened by Mrs. Billing slipping out of bed—regardless of draughts to her liege lord—and marching up and down the room with the visitor in her arms. He rose in the morning and dressed in ominous silence.

"I 'ope he didn't disturb you," said his wife, anxiously.

"You've done it," replied Mr. Billing. "You've upset everything now. Since I joined the Purnip lot everybody's took advantage of me; now I'm going to get some of my own back. You wouldn't ha' dreamt of behaving like this a few weeks ago."

"Oh, Joe!" said his wife, entreatingly; "and everybody's been so happy!"

"Except me," retorted Joe Billing. "You come down and get my breakfast ready. If I start early I shall catch Mr. Bill Ricketts on 'is way to work. And mind, if I find that steam-orgin 'ere when I come 'ome to-night you'll hear of it."

The Convert

He left the house with head erect and the light of battle in his eyes, and, meeting Mr. Ricketts at the corner, gave that justly aggrieved gentleman the surprise of his life. Elk Street thrilled to the fact that Mr. Billing had broken out again, and spoke darkly of what the evening might bring forth. Curious eyes followed his progress as he returned home from work, and a little later on the news was spread abroad that he was out and paying off old scores with an ardour that nothing could withstand.

"And wot about your change of 'art?" demanded one indignant matron, as her husband reached home five seconds ahead of Mr. Billing and hid in the scullery.

"It's changed agin," said Mr. Billing, simply.

He finished the evening in the Blue Lion, where he had one bar almost to himself, and, avoiding his wife's reproachful glance when he arrived home, procured some warm water and began to bathe his honourable scars.

"Mr. Purnip 'as been round with another gentleman," said his wife.

The Convert

Mr. Billing said "Oh!"

"Very much upset they was, and 'ope you'll go and see them," she continued.

Mr. Billing said "Oh!" again; and, after thinking the matter over, called next day at the Settlement and explained his position.

"It's all right for gentlemen like you," he said civilly. "But a man like me can't call his soul 'is own—or even 'is bedroom. Everybody takes advantage of 'im. Nobody ever gives *you* a punch, and, as for putting babies in your bedroom, they wouldn't dream of it."

He left amid expressions of general regret, turning a deaf ear to all suggestions about making another start, and went off exulting in his freedom.

His one trouble was Mr. Purnip, that estimable gentleman, who seemed to have a weird gift of meeting him at all sorts of times and places, never making any allusion to his desertion, but showing quite clearly by his manner that he still hoped for the return of the wanderer. It was awkward for a man of sensitive disposition,

The Convert

and Mr. Billing, before entering a street, got into the habit of peering round the corner first.

He pulled up suddenly one evening as he saw his tenacious friend, accompanied by a lady-member, some little distance ahead. Then he sprang forward with fists clenched as a passer-by, after scowling at Mr. Purnip, leaned forward and deliberately blew a mouthful of smoke into the face of his companion.

Mr. Billing stopped again and stood gaping with astonishment. The aggressor was getting up from the pavement, while Mr. Purnip, in an absolutely correct attitude, stood waiting for him. Mr. Billing in a glow of delight edged forward, and, with a few other fortunates, stood by watching one of the best fights that had ever been seen in the district. Mr. Purnip's foot-work was excellent, and the way he timed his blows made Mr. Billing's eyes moist with admiration.

It was over at last. The aggressor went limping off, and Mr. Purnip, wiping his bald head, picked up his battered and dusty hat from

The Convert

the roadway and brushed it on his sleeve. He turned with a start and a blush to meet the delighted gaze of Mr. Billing.

"I'm ashamed of myself," he murmured, brokenly—"ashamed."

"Ashamed!" exclaimed the amazed Mr. Billing. "Why, a pro couldn't ha' done better."

"Such an awful example," moaned the other. "All my good work here thrown away."

"Don't you believe it, sir," said Mr. Billing, earnestly. "As soon as this gets about you'll get more members than you want a'most. I'm coming back, for one."

Mr. Purnip turned and grasped his hand.

"I understand things now," said Mr. Billing, nodding sagely. "Turning the other cheek's all right so long as you don't do it always. If you don't let 'em know whether you are going to turn the other cheek or knock their blessed heads off, it's all right. 'Arf the trouble in the world is caused by letting people know too much."

Husbandry

Husbandry

DEALING with a man, said the night-watchman, thoughtfully, is as easy as a teetotaller walking along a nice wide pavement; dealing with a woman is like the same teetotaller, arter four or five whiskies, trying to get up a step that ain't there. If a man can't get 'is own way he eases 'is mind with a little nasty language, and then forgets all about it; if a woman can't get 'er own way she flies into a temper and reminds you of something you oughtn't to ha' done ten years ago. Wot a woman would do whose 'usband had never done anything wrong I can't think.

I remember a young feller telling me about a row he 'ad with 'is wife once. He 'adn't been married long and he talked as if the way she carried on was unusual. Fust of all, he said, she spoke to 'im in a cooing sort o' voice and pulled his moustache, then when he wouldn't

143

Husbandry

give way she worked herself up into a temper
and said things about 'is sister. Arter which
she went out o' the room and banged the
door so hard it blew down a vase off the
fireplace. Four times she came back to tell
'im other things she 'ad thought of, and then
she got so upset she 'ad to go up to bed and
lay down instead of getting his tea. When
that didn't do no good she refused her food,
and when 'e took her up toast and tea she
wouldn't look at it. Said she wanted to die.
He got quite uneasy till 'e came 'ome the next
night and found the best part of a loaf o' bread,
a quarter o' butter, and a couple o' chops he 'ad
got in for 'is supper had gorn; and then when
he said 'e was glad she 'ad got 'er appetite back
she turned round and said that he grudged 'er
the food she ate.

And no woman ever owned up as 'ow she
was wrong; and the more you try and prove it
to 'em the louder they talk about something
else. I know wot I'm talking about because a
woman made a mistake about me once, and

Husbandry

though she was proved to be in the wrong, and it was years ago, my missus shakes her 'ead about it to this day.

It was about eight years arter I 'ad left off going to sea and took up night-watching. A beautiful summer evening it was, and I was sitting by the gate smoking a pipe till it should be time to light up, when I noticed a woman who 'ad just passed turn back and stand staring at me. I've 'ad that sort o' thing before, and I went on smoking and looking straight in front of me. Fat middle-aged woman she was, wot 'ad lost her good looks and found others. She stood there staring and staring, and by and by she tries a little cough.

I got up very slow then, and, arter looking all round at the evening, without seeing 'er, I was just going to step inside and shut the wicket, when she came closer.

"Bill!" she ses, in a choking sort o' voice. "*Bill!*"

I gave her a look that made her catch 'er breath, and I was just stepping through the

Husbandry

wicket, when she laid hold of my coat and tried to hold me back.

"Do you know wot you're a-doing of?" I ses, turning on her.

"Oh, Bill dear," she ses, "don't talk to me like that. Do you want to break my 'art? Arter all these years!"

She pulled out a dirt-coloured pocket-'anker-cher and stood there dabbing her eyes with it. One eye at a time she dabbed, while she looked at me reproachful with the other. And arter eight dabs, four to each eye, she began to sob as if her 'art would break.

"Go away," I ses, very slow. "You can't stand making that noise outside my wharf. Go away and give somebody else a treat."

Afore she could say anything the potman from the Tiger, a nasty ginger-'aired little chap that nobody liked, come by and stopped to pat her on the back.

"There, there, don't take on, mother," he ses. "Wot's he been a-doing to you?"

"You get off 'ome," I ses, losing my temper.

146

Husbandry

"Wot d'ye mean trying to drag me into it? I've never seen the woman afore in my life."

"Oh, Bill!" ses the woman, sobbing louder than ever. "Oh! Oh! Oh!"

" 'Ow does she know your name, then?" ses the little beast of a potman.

I didn't answer him. I might have told 'im that there's about five million Bills in England, but I didn't. I stood there with my arms folded acrost my chest, and looked at him, superior.

"Where 'ave you been all this long, long time?" she ses, between her sobs. "Why did you leave your happy 'ome and your children wot loved you?"

The potman let off a whistle that you could have 'eard acrost the river, and as for me, I thought I should ha' dropped. To have a woman standing sobbing and taking my character away like that was a'most more than I could bear.

"Did he run away from you?" ses the potman.

"Ye-ye-yes," she ses. "He went off on a

Husbandry

vy'ge to China over nine years ago, and that's the last I saw of 'im till to-night.   A lady friend o' mine thought she reckernized 'im yesterday, and told me."

"I shouldn't cry over 'im," ses the potman, shaking his 'ead: "he ain't worth it.   If I was you I should just give 'im a bang or two over the 'ead with my umberella, and then give 'im in charge."

I stepped inside the wicket—backwards—and then I slammed it in their faces, and putting the key in my pocket, walked up the wharf. I knew it was no good standing out there argufying.   I felt sorry for the pore thing in a way.   If she really thought I was her 'usband, and she 'ad lost me—— I put one or two things straight and then, for the sake of distracting my mind, I 'ad a word or two with the skipper of the *John Henry*, who was leaning against the side of his ship, smoking.

"Wot's that tapping noise?" he ses, all of a sudden.   " 'Ark!"

I knew wot it was.   It was the handle of that

Husbandry

umberella 'ammering on the gate. I went cold all over, and then when I thought that the pot-man was most likely encouraging 'er to do it I began to boil.

"Somebody at the gate," ses the skipper.

"Aye, aye," I ses. "I know all about it."

I went on talking until at last the skipper asked me whether he was wandering in 'is mind, or whether I was. The mate came up from the cabin just then, and o' course *he* 'ad to tell me there was somebody knocking at the gate.

"Ain't you going to open it?" ses the skipper, staring at me.

"Let 'em ring," I ses, off-hand.

The words was 'ardly out of my mouth afore they did ring, and if they 'ad been selling muffins they couldn't ha' kept it up harder. And all the time the umberella was doing rat-a-tat tats on the gate, while a voice—much too loud for the potman's—started calling out: "Watchman ahoy!"

"They're calling you, Bill," ses the skipper.

"I ain't deaf," I ses, very cold.

Husbandry

"Well, I wish I was," ses the skipper. "It's fair making my ear ache. Why the blazes don't you do your dooty, and open the gate?"

"You mind your bisness and I'll mind mine," I ses. "I know wot I'm doing. It's just some silly fools 'aving a game with me, and I'm not going to encourage 'em."

"Game with you?" ses the skipper. "Ain't they got anything better than that to play with? Look 'ere, if you don't open that gate, I will."

"It's nothing to do with you," I ses. "You look arter your ship and I'll look arter my wharf. See? If you don't like the noise, go down in the cabin and stick your 'ead in a biscuit-bag."

To my surprise he took the mate by the arm and went, and I was just thinking wot a good thing it was to be a bit firm with people sometimes, when they came back dressed up in their coats and bowler-hats and climbed on to the wharf.

"Watchman!" ses the skipper, in a hoity-toity sort o' voice, "me and the mate is going

as far as Aldgate for a breath o' fresh air.
Open the gate."

I gave him a look that might ha' melted a
'art of stone, and all it done to 'im was to make
'im laugh.

"Hurry up," he ses. "It a'most seems to me
that there's somebody ringing the bell, and you
can let them in same time as you let us out. Is
it the bell, or is it my fancy, Joe?" he ses, turning to the mate.

They marched on in front of me with their
noses cocked in the air, and all the time the
noise at the gate got worse and worse. So far
as I could make out, there was quite a crowd
outside, and I stood there with the key in the
lock, trembling all over. Then I unlocked it
very careful, and put my hand on the skipper's
arm.

"Nip out quick," I ses, in a whisper.

"I'm in no hurry," ses the skipper. "Here!
Halloa, wot's up?"

It was like opening the door at a theatre, and
the fust one through was that woman, shoved

Husbandry

behind by the potman. Arter 'im came a carman, two big 'ulking brewers' draymen, a little
scrap of a woman with 'er bonnet cocked over
one eye, and a couple of dirty little boys.

"Wot is it?" ses the skipper, shutting the
wicket behind 'em. "A beanfeast?"

"This lady wants her 'usband," ses the potman, pointing at me. "He run away from her
nine years ago, and now he says he 'as never
seen 'er before. He ought to be 'ung."

"Bill," ses the skipper, shaking his silly 'ead
at me. "I can 'ardly believe it."

"It's all a pack o' silly lies," I ses, firing up.
"She's made a mistake."

"She made a mistake when she married you,"
ses the thin little woman. "If I was in 'er
shoes I'd take 'old of you and tear you limb
from limb."

"I don't want to hurt 'im, ma'am," ses the
other woman. "I on'y want him to come 'ome
to me and my five. Why, he's never seen the
youngest, little Annie. She's as like 'im as two
peas."

Husbandry

"Pore little devil," ses the carman.

"Look here!" I ses, "you clear off. All of you. 'Ow dare you come on to my wharf? If you aren't gone in two minutes I'll give you all in charge."

"Who to?" ses one of the draymen, sticking his face into mine. "You go 'ome to your wife and kids. Go on now, afore I put up my 'ands to you."

"That's the way to talk to 'im," ses the potman, nodding at 'em.

They all began to talk to me then and tell me wot I was to do, and wot they would do if I didn't. I couldn't get a word in edgeways. When I reminded the mate that when he was up in London 'e always passed himself off as a single man, 'e wouldn't listen; and when I asked the skipper whether 'is pore missus was blind, he on'y went on shouting at the top of 'is voice. It on'y showed me 'ow anxious most people are that everybody else should be good.

I thought they was never going to stop, and, if it 'adn't been for a fit of coughing, I don't

Husbandry

believe that the scraggy little woman *could* ha'
stopped. Arter one o' the draymen 'ad saved
her life and spoilt 'er temper by patting 'er on
the back with a hand the size of a leg o' mutton,
the carman turned to me and told me to tell the
truth, if it choked me.

"I have told you the truth," I ses. "She ses
I'm her 'usband and I say I ain't. Ow's she
going to prove it? Why should you believe
her, and not me?"

"*She's* got a truthful face," ses the carman.

"Look here!" ses the skipper, speaking very
slow, "I've got an idea, wot'll settle it p'raps.
You get outside," he ses, turning sharp on the
two little boys.

One o' the draymen 'elped 'em to go out, and
arf a minute arterwards a stone came over the
gate and cut the potman's lip open. Boys will
be boys.

"Now!" ses the skipper, turning to the
woman, and smiling with conceitedness. "Had
your 'usband got any marks on 'im? Birth-
mark, or moles, or anything of that sort?"

Husbandry

"I'm sure he *is* my 'usband," ses the woman, dabbing her eyes.

"Yes, yes," ses the skipper, "but answer my question. If you can tell us any marks your 'usband had, we can take Bill down into my cabin and——"

"You'll do WOT?" I ses, in a loud voice.

"You speak when you're spoke to," ses the carman. "It's got nothing to do with you."

"No, he ain't got no birthmarks," ses the woman, speaking very slow—and I could see she was afraid of making a mistake and losing me—"but he's got tattoo marks. He's got a mermaid tattooed on 'im."

"Where?" ses the skipper, a'most jumping.

I 'eld my breath. Five sailormen out of ten have been tattooed with mermaids, and I was one of 'em. When she spoke agin I thought I should ha' dropped.

"On 'is right arm," she ses, "unless he's 'ad it rubbed off."

"You can't rub out tattoo marks," ses the skipper.

Husbandry

They all stood looking at me as if they was waiting for something. I folded my arms—tight—and stared back at 'em.

"If you ain't this lady's 'usband," ses the skipper, turning to me, "you can take off your coat and prove it."

"And if you don't we'll take it off for you," ses the carman, coming a bit closer.

Arter that things 'appened so quick, I hardly knew whether I was standing on my 'ead or my heels. Both, I think. They was all on top o' me at once, and the next thing I can remember is sitting on the ground in my shirt-sleeves listening to the potman, who was making a fearful fuss because somebody 'ad bit his ear arf off. My coat was ripped up the back, and one of the draymen was holding up my arm and showing them all the mermaid, while the other struck matches so as they could see better."

"That's your 'usband right enough," he ses to the woman. "Take 'im."

"P'raps she'll carry 'im 'ome," I ses, very fierce and sarcastic.

Husbandry

"And we don't want none of your lip," ses the carman, who was in a bad temper because he 'ad got a fearful kick on the shin from somewhere.

I got up very slow and began to put my coat on again, and twice I 'ad to tell that silly woman that when I wanted her 'elp I'd let 'er know. Then I 'eard slow, heavy footsteps in the road outside, and, afore any of 'em could stop me, I was calling for the police.

I don't like policemen as a rule; they're too inquisitive, but when the wicket was pushed open and I saw a face with a helmet on it peeping in, I felt quite a liking for 'em.

"Wot's up?" ses the policeman, staring 'ard at my little party.

They all started telling 'im at once, and I should think if the potman showed him 'is ear once he showed it to 'im twenty times. He lost his temper and pushed it away at last, and the potman gave a 'owl that set my teeth on edge. I waited till they was all finished, and the policeman trying to get 'is hearing back, and then

Husbandry

I spoke up in a quiet way and told 'im to clear them all off of my wharf.

"They're trespassing," I ses, "all except the skipper and mate here. They belong to a little wash-tub that's laying alongside, and they're both as 'armless as they look."

It's wonderful wot a uniform will do. The policeman just jerked his 'ead and said "outside," and the men went out like a flock of sheep. The on'y man that said a word was the carman, who was in such a hurry that 'e knocked his bad shin against my foot as 'e went by. The thin little woman was passed out by the policeman in the middle of a speech she was making, and he was just going for the other, when the skipper stopped 'im.

"This lady is coming on my ship," he ses, puffing out 'is chest.

I looked at 'im, and then I turned to the policeman. "So long as she goes off my wharf, I don't mind where she goes," I ses. "The skipper's goings-on 'ave got nothing to do with me."

Husbandry

"Then she can foller him 'ome in the morning," ses the skipper. "Good night, watchman."

Him and the mate 'elped the silly old thing to the ship, and, arter I 'ad been round to the Bear's Head and fetched a pint for the policeman, I locked up and sat down to think things out; and the more I thought the worse they seemed. I've 'eard people say that if you have a clear conscience nothing can hurt you. They didn't know my missus.

I got up at last and walked on to the jetty, and the woman, wot was sitting on the deck of the *John Henry*, kept calling out: "Bill!" like a sick baa-lamb crying for its ma. I went back, and 'ad four pints at the Bear's Head, but it didn't seem to do me any good, and at last I went and sat down in the office to wait for morning.

It came at last, a lovely morning with a beautiful sunrise; and that woman sitting up wide awake, waiting to foller me 'ome. When I opened the gate at six o'clock she was there

Husbandry

with the mate and the skipper, waiting, and when I left at five minutes past she was trotting along beside me.

Twice I stopped and spoke to 'er, but it was no good. Other people stopped too, and I 'ad to move on agin; and every step was bringing me nearer to my house and the missus.

I turned into our street, arter passing it three times, and the first thing I saw was my missus standing on the doorstep 'aving a few words with the lady next door. Then she 'appened to look up and see us, just as that silly woman was trying to walk arm-in-arm.

Twice I knocked her 'and away, and then, right afore my wife and the party next door, she put her arm round my waist. By the time I got to the 'ouse my legs was trembling so I could hardly stand, and when I got into the passage I 'ad to lean up against the wall for a bit.

"Keep 'er out," I ses.

"Wot do you want?" ses my missus, trem-

RIGHT AFORE MY WIFE AND THE PARTY NEXT DOOR SHE PUT HER
ARM ROUND MY WAIST.

Husbandry

bling with passion. "Wot do you think you're doing?"

"I want my 'usband, Bill," ses the woman.

My missus put her 'and to her throat and came in without a word, and the woman follered 'er. If I hadn't kept my presence o' mind and shut the door two or three more would 'ave come in too.

I went into the kitchen about ten minutes arterwards to see 'ow they was getting on. Besides which they was both calling for me.

"Now then!" ses my missus, who was leaning up against the dresser with 'er arms folded, "wot 'ave you got to say for yourself walking in as bold as brass with this hussy?"

"Bill!" ses the woman, "did you hear wot she called me?"

She spoke to me like that afore my wife, and in two minutes they was at it, hammer and tongs.

Fust of all they spoke about each other, and then my missus started speaking about me. She's got a better memory than most people, because she can remember things that never 'appened, and every time I coughed she turned on me like a tiger.

"And as for you," she ses, turning to the woman, "if you did marry 'im you should ha' made sure that he 'adn't got a wife already."

"He married me fust," ses the woman.

"When?" ses my wife. "Wot was the date?"

"Wot was the date you married 'im?" ses the other one.

They stood looking at each other like a couple o' game-cocks, and I could see as plain as a pike-staff 'ow frightened both of 'em was o' losing me.

"Look here!" I ses at last, to my missus, "talk sense. 'Ow could I be married to 'er? When I was at sea I was at sea, and when I was ashore I was with you."

"Did you use to go down to the ship to see 'im off?" ses the woman.

"No," ses my wife. "I'd something better to do."

Husbandry

"Neither did I," ses the woman. "P'raps that's where we both made a mistake."

"You get out of my 'ouse!" ses my missus, very sudden. "Go on, afore I put you out."

"Not without my Bill," ses the woman. "If you lay a finger on me I'll scream the house down."

"You brought her 'ere," ses my wife, turning to me, "now you can take 'er away?"

"I didn't bring 'er," I ses. "She follered me."

"Well, she can foller you agin," she ses. "Go on!" she ses, trembling all over. "Git out afore I start on you."

I was in such a temper that I daren't trust myself to stop. I just gave 'er one look, and then I drew myself up and went out. 'Alf the fools in our street was standing in front of the 'ouse, 'umming like bees, but I took no notice. I held my 'ead up and walked through them with that woman trailing arter me.

I was in such a state of mind that I went on like a man in a dream. If it *had* ha' been a

163

Husbandry

dream I should ha' pushed 'er under an omni-
bus, but you can't do things like that in real
life.

"Penny for your thoughts, Bill," she ses.

I didn't answer her.

"Why don't you speak to me?" she ses.

"You don't know wot you're asking for," I
ses.

I was hungry and sleepy, and 'ow I was going to get through the day I couldn't think. I
went into a pub and 'ad a couple o' pints o'
stout and a crust o' bread and cheese for brekfuss. I don't know wot she 'ad, but when the
barman tried to take for it out o' my money, I
surprised 'im.

We walked about till I was ready to drop.
Then we got to Victoria Park, and I 'ad no
sooner got on to the grass than I laid down and
went straight off to sleep. It was two o'clock
when I woke, and, arter a couple o' pork-pies
and a pint or two, I sat on a seat in the Park
smoking, while she kep' dabbing 'er eyes agin
and asking me to come 'ome.

Husbandry

At five o'clock I got up to go back to the wharf, and, taking no notice of 'er, I walked into the street and jumped on a 'bus that was passing. She jumped too, and, arter the conductor had 'elped 'er up off of 'er knees and taken her arms away from his waist, I'm blest if he didn't turn on me and ask me why I 'adn't left her at 'ome.

We got to the wharf just afore six. The *John Henry* 'ad gorn, but the skipper 'ad done all the 'arm he could afore he sailed, and, if I 'adn't kept my temper, I should ha' murdered arf a dozen of 'em.

The woman wanted to come on to the wharf, but I 'ad a word or two with one o' the foremen, who owed me arf-a-dollar, and he made that all right.

"We all 'ave our faults, Bill," he ses as 'e went out, "and I suppose she was better looking once upon a time?"

I didn't answer 'im. I shut the wicket arter 'im, quick, and turned the key, and then I went on with my work. For a long time everything

165

Husbandry

was as quiet as the grave, and then there came just one little pull at the bell. Five minutes arterwards there was another.

I thought it was that woman, but I 'ad to make sure. When it came the third time I crept up to the gate.

"Halloa!" I ses. "Who is it?"

"Me, darling," ses a voice I reckernized as the potman's. "Your missus wants to come in and sit down."

I could 'ear several people talking, and it seemed to me there was quite a crowd out there, and by and by that bell was going like mad. Then people started kicking the gate, and shouting, but I took no notice until, presently, it left off all of a sudden, and I 'eard a loud voice asking what it was all about. I suppose there was about fifty of 'em all telling it at once, and then there was the sound of a fist on the gate.

"Who is it?" I ses.

"Police," ses the voice.

I opened the wicket then and looked out. A

Husbandry

couple o' policemen was standing by the gate and arf the riff-raff of Wapping behind 'em.

"Wot's all this about?" ses one o' the policemen.

I shook my 'ead. "Ask me another," I ses.

"Your missus is causing a disturbance," he ses.

"She's not my missus," I ses; "she's a complete stranger to me."

"And causing a crowd to collect and refusing to go away," ses the other policeman.

"That's your business," I ses. "It's nothing to do with me."

They talked to each other for a moment, and then they spoke to the woman. I didn't 'ear wot she said, but I saw her shake her 'ead, and a'most direckly arterwards she was marching away between the two policemen with the crowd follering and advising 'er where to kick 'em.

I was a bit worried at fust—not about her—and then I began to think that p'raps it was the best thing that could have 'appened.

Husbandry

I went 'ome in the morning with a load lifted off my mind; but I 'adn't been in the 'ouse two seconds afore my missus started to put it on agin. Fust of all she asked me 'ow I dared to come into the 'ouse, and then she wanted to know wot I meant by leaving her at 'ome and going out for the day with another woman.

"You told me to," I ses

"Oh, yes," she ses, trembling with temper. "You always do wot I tell you, don't you? Always 'ave, especially when it's anything you like."

She fetched a bucket o' water and scrubbed the kitchen while I was having my brekfuss, but I kept my eye on 'er, and, the moment she 'ad finished, I did the perlite and emptied the bucket for 'er, to prevent mistakes.

I read about the case in the Sunday paper, and I'm thankful to say my name wasn't in it. All the magistrate done was to make 'er promise that she wouldn't do it again, and then he let 'er go. I should ha' felt more comfortable if he 'ad given 'er five years, but, as it turned

Husbandry

out, it didn't matter. Her 'usband happened to read it, and, whether 'e was tired of living alone, or whether he was excited by 'earing that she 'ad got a little general shop, 'e went back to her.

The fust I knew about it was they came round to the wharf to see me. He 'ad been a fine-looking chap in 'is day, and even then 'e was enough like me for me to see 'ow she 'ad made the mistake; and all the time she was telling me 'ow it 'appened, he was looking me up and down and sniffing.

"'Ave you got a cold?" I ses, at last.

"Wot's that got to do with you?" he ses. "Wot do you mean by walking out with my wife? That's what I've come to talk about."

For a moment I thought that his bad luck 'ad turned 'is brain. "You've got it wrong," I ses, as soon as I could speak. "She walked out with me."

"Cos she thought you was her 'usband," he ses, "but you didn't think you was me, did you?"

" 'Course I didn't," I ses.

Husbandry

"Then 'ow dare you walk out with 'er?" he ses.

"Look 'ere!" I ses. "You get off 'ome as quick as you like. I've 'ad about enough of your family. Go on, hook it."

Afore I could put my 'ands up he 'it me hard in the mouth, and the next moment we was at it as 'ard as we could go. Nearly every time I hit 'im he wasn't there, and every time 'e hit me I wished I hadn't ha' been. When I said I had 'ad enough, 'e contradicted me and kept on, but he got tired of it at last, and, arter telling me wot he would do if I ever walked 'is wife out agin, they went off like a couple o' love-birds.

By the time I got 'ome next morning my eyes was so swelled up I could 'ardly see, and my nose wouldn't let me touch it. I was so done up I could 'ardly speak, but I managed to tell my missus about it arter I had 'ad a cup o' tea. Judging by her face anybody might ha' thought I was telling 'er something funny, and, when I 'ad finished, she looks up at the ceiling and ses:

"I 'ope it'll be a lesson to you," she ses.

Family Cares

Family Cares

MR. JERNSHAW, who was taking the opportunity of a lull in business to weigh out pound packets of sugar, knocked his hands together and stood waiting for the order of the tall bronzed man who had just entered the shop—a well-built man of about forty—who was regarding him with blue eyes set in quizzical wrinkles.

"What, Harry!" exclaimed Mr. Jernshaw, in response to the wrinkles. "Harry Barrett!"

"That's me," said the other, extending his hand. "The rolling stone come home covered with moss."

Mr. Jernshaw, somewhat excited, shook hands, and led the way into the little parlour behind the shop.

"Fifteen years," said Mr. Barrett, sinking into a chair, "and the old place hasn't altered a bit."

Family Cares

"Smithson told me he had let that house in Webb Street to a Barrett," said the grocer, regarding him, "but I never thought of you. I suppose you've done well, then?"

Mr. Barrett nodded. "Can't grumble," he said modestly. "I've got enough to live on. Melbourne's all right, but I thought I'd come home for the evening of my life."

"Evening!" repeated his friend.

"Forty-three," said Mr. Barrett, gravely. "I'm getting on."

"You haven't changed much," said the grocer, passing his hand through his spare grey whiskers. "Wait till you have a wife and seven youngsters. Why, boots alone——"

Mr. Barrett uttered a groan intended for sympathy. "Perhaps you could help me with the furnishing," he said, slowly. "I've never had a place of my own before, and I don't know much about it."

"Anything I can do," said his friend. "Better not get much yet; you might marry, and my taste mightn't be hers."

Family Cares

Mr. Barrett laughed. "I'm not marrying," he said, with conviction.

"Seen anything of Miss Prentice yet?" inquired Mr. Jernshaw.

"No," said the other, with a slight flush. "Why?"

"She's still single," said the grocer.

"What of it?" demanded Mr. Barrett, with warmth. "What of it?"

"Nothing," said Mr. Jernshaw, slowly. "Nothing; only I——"

"Well?" said the other, as he paused.

"I—there was an idea that you went to Australia to—to better your condition," murmured the grocer. "That—that you were not in a position to marry—that——"

"Boy and girl nonsense," said Mr. Barrett, sharply. "Why, it's fifteen years ago. I don't suppose I should know her if I saw her. Is her mother alive?"

"Rather!" said Mr. Jernshaw, with emphasis. "Louisa is something like what her mother was when you went away."

Family Cares

Mr. Barrett shivered.

"But you'll see for yourself," continued the other. "You'll have to go and see them. They'll wonder you haven't been before."

"Let 'em wonder," said the embarrassed Mr. Barrett. "I shall go and see all my old friends in their turn; casual-like. You might let 'em hear that I've been to see you before seeing them, and then, if they're thinking any nonsense, it'll be a hint. I'm stopping in town while the house is being decorated; next time I come down I'll call and see somebody else."

"That'll be another hint," assented Mr. Jernshaw. "Not that hints are much good to Mrs. Prentice."

"We'll see," said Mr. Barrett.

In accordance with his plan his return to his native town was heralded by a few short visits at respectable intervals. A sort of human butterfly, he streaked rapidly across one or two streets, alighted for half an hour to resume an old friendship, and then disappeared again. Having given at least half-a-dozen hints of this

Family Cares

kind, he made a final return to Ramsbury and entered into occupation of his new house.

"It does you credit, Jernshaw," he said, gratefully. "I should have made a rare mess of it without your help."

"It looks very nice," admitted his friend. "Too nice."

"That's all nonsense," said the owner, irritably.

"All right," said Mr. Jernshaw. "I don't know the sex, then, that's all. If you think that you're going to keep a nice house like this all to yourself, you're mistaken. It's a *home;* and where there's a home a woman comes in, somehow."

Mr. Barrett grunted his disbelief.

"I give you four days," said Mr. Jernshaw.

As a matter of fact, Mrs. Prentice and her daughter came on the fifth. Mr. Barrett, who was in an easy-chair, wooing slumber with a handkerchief over his head, heard their voices at the front door and the cordial invitation of

Family Cares

his housekeeper. They entered the room as he sat hastily smoothing his rumpled hair.

"Good afternoon," he said, shaking hands.

Mrs. Prentice returned the greeting in a level voice, and, accepting a chair, gazed around the room.

"Nice weather," said Mr. Barrett.

"Very," said Mrs. Prentice.

"It's—it's quite a pleasure to see you again," said Mr. Barrett.

"We thought we should have seen you before," said Mrs. Prentice, "but I told Louisa that no doubt you were busy, and wanted to surprise her. I like the carpet; don't you, Louisa?"

Miss Prentice said she did.

"The room is nice and airy," said Mrs. Prentice, "but it's a pity you didn't come to me before deciding. I could have told you of a better house for the same money."

"I'm very well satisfied with this," said Mr. Barrett. "It's all *I* want."

"It's well enough," conceded Mrs. Prentice,

Family Cares

amiably. "And how have you been all these years?"

Mr. Barrett, with some haste, replied that his health and spirits had been excellent.

"You look well," said Mrs. Prentice. "Neither of you seem to have changed much," she added, looking from him to her daughter. "And I think you did quite well not to write. I think it was much the best."

Mr. Barrett sought for a question: a natural, artless question, that would neutralize the hideous suggestion conveyed by this remark, but it eluded him. He sat and gazed in growing fear at Mrs. Prentice.

"I—I couldn't write," he said at last, in desperation; "my wife——"

"Your *what?*" exclaimed Mrs. Prentice, loudly.

"Wife," said Mr. Barrett, suddenly calm now that he had taken the plunge. "She wouldn't have liked it."

Mrs. Prentice tried to control her voice. "I never heard you were married!" she gasped. "Why isn't she here?"

179

Family Cares

"We couldn't agree," said the veracious Mr. Barrett. "She was very difficult; so I left the children with her and——"

"Chil——" said Mrs. Prentice, and paused, unable to complete the word.

"Five," said Mr. Barrett, in tones of resignation. "It was rather a wrench, parting with them, especially the baby. He got his first tooth the day I left."

The information fell on deaf ears. Mrs. Prentice, for once in her life thoroughly at a loss, sat trying to collect her scattered faculties. She had come out prepared for a hard job, but not an impossible one. All things considered, she took her defeat with admirable composure.

"I have no doubt it is much the best thing for the children to remain with their mother," she said, rising.

"Much the best," agreed Mr. Barrett.

"Whatever she is like," continued the old lady. "Are you ready, Louisa?"

Mr. Barrett followed them to the door, and

Family Cares

then, returning to the room, watched, with glad eyes, their progress up the street.

"Wonder whether she'll keep it to herself?" he muttered.

His doubts were set at rest next day. All Ramsbury knew by then of his matrimonial complications, and seemed anxious to talk about them; complications which tended to increase until Mr. Barrett wrote out a list of his children's names and ages and learnt it off by heart.

Relieved of the attentions of the Prentice family, he walked the streets a free man; and it was counted to him for righteousness that he never said a hard word about his wife. She had her faults, he said, but they were many thousand miles away, and he preferred to forget them. And he added, with some truth, that he owed her a good deal.

For a few months he had no reason to alter his opinion. Thanks to his presence of mind, the Prentice family had no terrors for him. Heart-whole and fancy free, he led the easy life

Family Cares

of a man of leisure, a condition of things suddenly upset by the arrival of Miss Grace Lindsay to take up a post at the elementary school. Mr. Barrett succumbed almost at once, and, after a few encounters in the street and meetings at mutual friends', went to unbosom himself to Mr. Jernshaw.

"What has she got to do with you?" demanded that gentleman.

"I—I'm rather struck with her," said Mr. Barrett.

"Struck with her?" repeated his friend, sharply. "I'm surprised at you. You've no business to think of such things."

"Why not?" demanded Mr. Barrett, in tones that were sharper still.

"Why not?" repeated the other. "Have you forgotten your wife and children?"

Mr. Barrett, who, to do him justice, *had* forgotten, fell back in his chair and sat gazing at him, open-mouthed.

"You're in a false position—in a way," said Mr. Jernshaw, sternly.

Family Cares

"False is no name for it," said Mr. Barrett, huskily. "What am I to do?"

"*Do?*" repeated the other, staring at him. "Nothing! Unless, perhaps, you send for your wife and children. I suppose, in any case, you would have to have the little ones if anything happened to her?"

Mr. Barrett grinned ruefully.

"Think it over," said Mr. Jernshaw.

"I will," said the other, heartily.

He walked home deep in thought. He was a kindly man, and he spent some time thinking out the easiest death for Mrs. Barrett. He decided at last upon heart-disease, and a fortnight later all Ramsbury knew of the letter from Australia conveying the mournful intelligence. It was generally agreed that the mourning and the general behaviour of the widower left nothing to be desired.

"She's at peace at last," he said, solemnly, to Jernshaw.

"I believe you killed her," said his friend.

Mr. Barrett started violently.

Family Cares

"I mean your leaving broke her heart," explained the other.

Mr. Barrett breathed easily again.

"It's your duty to look after the children," said Jernshaw, firmly. "And I'm not the only one that thinks so."

"They are with their grandfather and grandmother," said Mr. Barrett.

Mr. Jernshaw sniffed.

"And four uncles and five aunts," added Mr. Barrett, triumphantly.

"Think how they would brighten up your house," said Mr. Jernshaw.

His friend shook his head. "It wouldn't be fair to their grandmother," he said, decidedly. "Besides, Australia wants population."

He found to his annoyance that Mr. Jernshaw's statement that he was not alone in his views was correct. Public opinion seemed to expect the arrival of the children, and one citizen even went so far as to recommend a girl he knew, as nurse.

Ramsbury understood at last that his de-

Family Cares

cision was final, and, observing his attentions to the new schoolmistress, flattered itself that it had discovered the reason. It is possible that Miss Lindsay shared their views, but if so she made no sign, and on the many occasions on which she met Mr. Barrett on her way to and from school greeted him with frank cordiality. Even when he referred to his loneliness, which he did frequently, she made no comment.

He went into half-mourning at the end of two months, and a month later bore no outward signs of his loss. Added to that his step was springy and his manner youthful. Miss Lindsay was twenty-eight, and he persuaded himself that, sexes considered, there was no disparity worth mentioning.

He was only restrained from proposing by a question of etiquette. Even a shilling book on the science failed to state the interval that should elapse between the death of one wife and the negotiations for another. It preferred instead to give minute instructions with regard

Family Cares

to the eating of asparagus. In this dilemma he consulted Jernshaw.

"Don't know, I'm sure," said that gentleman; "besides, it doesn't matter."

"Doesn't matter?" repeated Mr. Barrett. "Why not?"

"Because I think Tillett is paying her attentions," was the reply. "He's ten years younger than you are, and a bachelor. A girl would naturally prefer him to a middle-aged widower with five children."

"In Australia," the other reminded him.

"Man for man, bachelor for bachelor," said Mr. Jernshaw, regarding him, "she might prefer you; as things are——"

"I shall ask her," said Mr. Barrett, doggedly. "I was going to wait a bit longer, but if there's any chance of her wrecking her prospects for life by marrying that tailor's dummy it's my duty to risk it—for her sake. I've seen him talking to her twice myself, but I never thought he'd dream of such a thing."

Apprehension and indignation kept him

186

Family Cares

awake half the night, but when he arose next morning it was with the firm resolve to put his fortune to the test that day. At four o'clock he changed his neck-tie for the third time, and at ten past sallied out in the direction of the school. He met Miss Lindsay just coming out, and, after a well-deserved compliment to the weather, turned and walked with her.

"I was hoping to meet you," he said, slowly.

"Yes?" said the girl.

"I—I have been feeling rather lonely to-day," he continued.

"You often do," said Miss Lindsay, guardedly.

"It gets worse and worse," said Mr. Barrett, sadly.

"I think I know what is the matter with you," said the girl, in a soft voice; "you have got nothing to do all day, and you live alone, except for your housekeeper."

Mr. Barrett assented with some eagerness, and stole a hopeful glance at her.

Family Cares

"You—you miss something," continued Miss Lindsay, in a faltering voice.

"I do," said Mr. Barrett, with ardour.

"You miss"—the girl made an effort—"you miss the footsteps and voices of your little children."

Mr. Barrett stopped suddenly in the street, and then, with a jerk, went blindly on.

"I've never spoken of it before because it's your business, not mine," continued the girl. I wouldn't have spoken now, but when you referred to your loneliness I thought perhaps you didn't realize the cause of it."

Mr. Barrett walked on in silent misery.

"Poor little motherless things!" said Miss Lindsay, softly. "Motherless and — fatherless."

"Better for them," said Mr. Barrett, finding his voice at last.

"It almost looks like it," said Miss Lindsay, with a sigh.

Mr. Barrett tried to think clearly, but the circumstances were hardly favourable. "Suppose," he said, speaking very slowly, "suppose I wanted to get married?"

Miss Lindsay started. "What, again?" she said, with an air of surprise.

"How could I ask a girl to come and take over five children?"

"No woman that was worth having would let little children be sacrificed for her sake," said Miss Lindsay, decidedly.

"Do you think anybody would marry me with five children?" demanded Mr. Barrett.

"She might," said the girl, edging away from him a little. "It depends on the woman."

"Would—you, for instance?" said Mr. Barrett, desperately.

Miss Lindsay shrank still farther away. "I don't know; it would depend upon circumstances," she murmured.

"I will write and send for them," said Mr. Barrett, significantly.

Miss Lindsay made no reply. They had arrived at her gate by this time, and, with a hurried handshake, she disappeared indoors.

Family Cares

Mr. Barrett, somewhat troubled in mind, went home to tea.

He resolved, after a little natural hesitation, to drown the children, and reproached himself bitterly for not having disposed of them at the same time as their mother. Now he would have to go through another period of mourning and the consequent delay in pressing his suit. Moreover, he would have to allow a decent interval between his conversation with Miss Lindsay and their untimely end.

The news of the catastrophe arrived two or three days before the return of the girl from her summer holidays. She learnt it in the first half-hour from her landlady, and sat in a dazed condition listening to a description of the grief-stricken father and the sympathy extended to him by his fellow-citizens. It appeared that nothing had passed his lips for two days.

"Shocking!" said Miss Lindsay, briefly. "Shocking!"

An instinctive feeling that the right and proper thing to do was to nurse his grief in soli-

SHE LEARNT THE NEWS IN THE FIRST HALF-HOUR FROM HER
LANDLADY.

Family Cares

tude kept Mr. Barrett out of her way for nearly a week. When she did meet him she received a limp handshake and a greeting in a voice from which all hope seemed to have departed.

"I am very sorry," she said, with a sort of measured gentleness.

Mr. Barrett, in his hushed voice, thanked her.

"I am all alone now," he said, pathetically. "There is nobody now to care whether I live or die."

Miss Lindsay did not contradict him.

"How did it happen?" she inquired, after they had gone some distance in silence.

"They were out in a sailing-boat," said Mr. Barrett; "the boat capsized in a puff of wind, and they were all drowned."

"Who was in charge of them?" inquired the girl, after a decent interval.

"Boatman," replied the other.

"How did you hear?"

"I had a letter from one of my sisters-in-law, Charlotte," said Mr. Barrett. "A most affecting letter. Poor Charlotte was like a second mother to them. She'll never be the same woman again. Never!"

"I should like to see the letter," said Miss Lindsay, musingly.

Mr. Barrett suppressed a start. "I should like to show it to you," he said, "but I'm afraid I have destroyed it. It made me shudder every time I looked at it."

"It's a pity," said the girl, dryly. "I should have liked to see it. I've got my own idea about the matter. Are you sure she was very fond of them?"

"She lived only for them," said Mr. Barrett, in a rapt voice.

"Exactly. I don't believe they are drowned at all," said Miss Lindsay, suddenly. "I believe you have had all this terrible anguish for nothing. It's too cruel."

Mr. Barrett stared at her in anxious amazement.

"I see it all now," continued the girl. "Their Aunt Charlotte was devoted to them. She always had the fear that some day you would return and claim them, and to prevent that she invented the story of their death."

"Charlotte is the most truthful woman that ever breathed," said the distressed Mr. Barrett.

Miss Lindsay shook her head. "You are like all other honourable, truthful people," she said, looking at him gravely. "You can't imagine anybody else telling a falsehood. I don't believe you could tell one if you tried."

Mr. Barrett gazed about him with the despairing look of a drowning mariner.

"I'm certain I'm right," continued the girl. "I can see Charlotte exulting in her wickedness. *Why!*"

"What's the matter?" inquired Mr. Barrett, greatly worried.

"I've just thought of it," said Miss Lindsay. "She's told you that your children are drowned, and she has probably told them you are dead. A woman like that would stick at nothing to gain her ends."

Family Cares

"You don't know Charlotte," said Mr. Barrett, feebly.

"I think I do," was the reply. "However, we'll make sure. I suppose you've got friends in Melbourne?"

"A few," said Mr. Barrett, guardedly.

"Come down to the post-office and cable to one of them."

Mr. Barrett hesitated. "I'll write," he said, slowly. "It's an awkward thing to cable; and there's no hurry. I'll write to Jack Adams, I think."

"It's no good writing," said Miss Lindsay, firmly. "You ought to know that."

"Why not?" demanded the other.

"Because, you foolish man," said the girl, calmly, "before your letter got there, there would be one from Melbourne saying that he had been choked by a fish-bone, or died of measles, or something of that sort."

Mr. Barrett, hardly able to believe his ears, stopped short and looked at her. The girl's eyes were moist with mirth and her lips trembling. He put out his hand and took her wrist in a strong grip.

"That's all right," he said, with a great gasp of relief. "*Phew!* At one time I thought I had lost you."

"By heart-disease, or drowning?" inquired Miss Lindsay, softly.

The Winter Offensive

The Winter Offensive

Aug. 29, 1916.—We returned from the sea to find our house still our own, and the military still in undisputed possession of the remains of the grass in the fields of Berkhamsted Place. As in previous years, it was impossible to go in search of wild-flowers without stumbling over sleeping members of the Inns of Court; but war is war, and we grumble as little as possible.

Sept. 28.—Unpleasant rumours to the effect that several members of the Inns of Court had attributed cases of curvature of the spine to sleeping on ground that had been insufficiently rolled. Also that they had been heard to smack their lips and speak darkly of feather-

199

beds. Respected neighbour of gloomy disposition said that if Pharaoh were still alive he could suggest an eleventh plague to him beside which frogs and flies were an afternoon's diversion.

Oct. 3.—Householders of Berkhamsted busy mending bedsteads broken by last year's billets, and buying patent taps for their beer-barrels.

Oct. 15.—Informed that a representative of the Army wished to see me. Instead of my old friend Q.M.S. Beddem, who generally returns to life at this time of year, found that it was an officer of magnificent presence and two pips. A fine figure of a man, with a great resemblance to the late lamented Bismarck, minus the moustache and the three hairs on the top of the head. Asked him to be seated. He selected a chair that was all arms and legs and no hips to speak of and crushed himself into it. After which he unfastened his belt and "swelled wisibly afore my werry eyes." Said that his name was True Born and asked if it made any difference to me whether I had one officer or half-a-dozen men

The Winter Offensive

billeted on me. Said that he was the officer, and that as the rank-and-file were not allowed to pollute the same atmosphere, thought I should score. After a mental review of all I could remember of the *Weights and Measures Table,* accepted him. He bade a lingering farewell to the chair, and departed.

Oct. 16.—Saw Q.M.S. Beddem on the other side of the road and gave him an absolutely new thrill by crossing to meet him. Asked diffidently—as diffidently as he could, that is—how many men my house would hold. Replied eight —or ten at a pinch. He gave me a surprised and beaming smile and whipped out a huge note-book. Informed him with as much regret as I could put into a voice not always under perfect control, that I had already got an officer. Q.M.S., favouring me with a look very appropriate to the Devil's Own, turned on his heel and set off in pursuit of a lady-billetee, pulling up short on the threshold of the baby-linen shop in which she took refuge. Left him on guard with a Casabianca-like look on his face.

The Winter Offensive

Nov. 1.—Lieut. True Born took up his quarters with us. Gave him my dressing-room for bedchamber. Was awakened several times in the night by what I took to be Zeppelins, flying low.

Nov. 2.—Lieut. True Born offered to bet me five pounds to twenty that the war would be over by 1922.

Nov. 3.—Offered to teach me auction-bridge.

Nov. 4.—Asked me whether I could play "shove ha'penny."

Nov. 10.—Lieut. True Born gave one of the regimental horses a riding-lesson. Came home grumpy and went to bed early.

Nov. 13. — Another riding-lesson. Overheard him asking one of the maids whether there was such a thing as a water-bed in the house.

Nov. 17.—Complained bitterly of horse-copers. Said that his poor mount was discovered to be suffering from saddle-soreness, broken wind, splints, weak hocks, and two bones of the neck out of place.

The Winter Offensive

Dec. 9.—7 *p.m.*—One of last year's billets, Private Merited, on leave from a gunnery course, called to see me and to find out whether his old bed had improved since last year. Left his motor-bike in the garage, and the smell in front of the dining-room window.

8 to 12 *p.m.* — Sat with Private Merited, listening to Lieut. True Born on the mistakes of Wellington.

12.5 *a.m.*—Rose to go to bed. Was about to turn out gas in hall when I discovered the lieutenant standing with his face to the wall playing pat-a-cake with it. Gave him three-parts of a tumbler of brandy. Said he felt better and went upstairs. Arrived in his bed-room, he looked about him carefully, and then, with a superb sweep of his left arm, swept the best Chippendale looking-glass in the family off the dressing table and dived face downwards to the floor, missing death and the corner of the chest of drawers by an inch.

12:15 *a.m.*—Rolled him on to his back and got his feet on the bed. They fell off again as

The Winter Offensive

soon as they were cleaner than the quilt. The lieutenant, startled by the crash, opened his eyes and climbed into bed unaided.

12.20 *a.m.*—Sent Private Merited for the M.O., Captain Geranium.

12.25 *a.m.*—Mixed a dose of brandy and castor-oil in a tumbler. Am told it slips down like an oyster that way—bad oyster, I should think. Lieut. True Born jibbed. Reminded him that England expects that every man will take his castor-oil. Reply unprintable. Apologized a moment later. Said that his mind was wandering and that he thought he was a colonel. Reassured him.

12.40 *a.m.*—Private Merited returned with the M.O. Latter nicely dressed in musical-comedy pyjamas of ravishing hue, and greatcoat, with rose-tinted feet thrust into red morocco slippers. Held consultation and explained my treatment. M.O. much impressed, anxious to know whether I was a doctor. Told him "No," but that I knew all the ropes. First give patient castor-oil, then diet him and call

The Winter Offensive

every day to make sure that he doesn't like his food. After that, if he shows signs of getting well too soon, give him a tonic. . . . M.O. stuffy.

Dec. 10.—M.O. diagnosed attack as due to something which True Born believes to be tobacco, with which he disinfects the house, the mess-sheds, and the streets of Berkhamsted.

Dec. 11. — True Born, shorn of thirteen pipes a day out of sixteen, disparages the whole race of M.O.'s.

Dec. 14.—He obtains leave to attend wedding of a great-aunt and ransacks London for a specialist who advocates strong tobacco.

Dec. 15. — He classes specialists with M.O.'s. Is surprised (and apparently disappointed) that, so far, the breaking of the looking-glass has brought me no ill-luck. Feel somewhat uneasy myself until glass is repaired by local cabinet-maker.

Jan. 10, 1917.—Lieut. True Born starts to break in another horse.

Feb. 1.—Horse broken.

The Winter Offensive

March 3.—Running short of tobacco, go to my billet's room and try a pipe of his. Take all the remedies except the castor-oil.

April 4, 8.30 *a.m.*—Awakened by an infernal crash and discover that my poor looking-glass is in pieces again on the floor. True Born explains that its position, between the open door and the open window, was too much for it. Don't believe a word of it. Shall believe to my dying day that it burst in a frantic but hopeless attempt to tell Lieut. True Born the truth, the whole truth, and nothing but the truth.

April 6.—The lieutenant watching for some sign of misfortune to me. Says that I can't break a mirror twice without ill-luck following it. *Me!*

April 9.—Lieut. True Born comes up to me with a face full of conflicting emotions. "Your ill-luck has come at last," he says with gloomy satisfaction. "We go under canvas on the 23rd. *You are losing me!*"

The Substitute

The Substitute

THE night watchman had just returned to the office fire after leaving it to attend a ring at the wharf bell. He sat for some time puffing fiercely at his pipe and breathing heavily.

"Boys!" he said, at last. "That's the third time this week, and yet if I was to catch one and skin 'im alive I suppose I should get into trouble over it. Even 'is own father and mother would make a fuss, most like. Some people have boys, and other people 'ave the trouble of 'em. Our street's full of 'em, and the way they carry on would make a monkey-'ouse ashamed of itself. The man next door to me's got seven of 'em, and when I spoke to 'im friendly about it over a pint one night, he put the blame on 'is wife.

"The worst boy I ever knew used to be office-boy in this 'ere office, and I can't understand

now why I wasn't 'ung for him.   Undersized
little chap he was, with a face the colour o' bad
pie-crust, and two little black eyes like shoe-
buttons.   To see 'im with his little white cuffs,
and a stand-up collar, and a little black bow,
and a little bowler-'at, was enough to make a
cat laugh.   I told 'im so one day, and arter that
we knew where we was.   Both of us.

"By rights he ought to 'ave left the office
at six—just my time for coming on.   As it was,
he used to stay late, purtending to work 'ard so
as to get a rise.   Arter all the clerks 'ad gorn
'ome he used to sit perched up on a stool yards
too 'igh for him, with one eye on the ledger and
the other looking through the winder at me.   I
remember once going off for 'arf a pint, and
when I come back I found 'im with a policeman,
two carmen, and all the hands off of the *Maid
Marian*, standing on the edge of the jetty, waiting for me to come up.   He said that, not finding me on the wharf, 'e made sure that I must
'ave tumbled overboard, as he felt certain that
I wouldn't neglect my dooty while there was

The Substitute

breath in my body; but 'e was sorry to find 'e was mistook. He stood there talking like a little clergyman, until one of the carmen knocked his 'at over 'is eyes, and then he forgot 'imself for a bit.

"Arter that I used to wait until he 'ad gorn afore I 'ad my arf-pint. I didn't want my good name taken away, and I had to be careful, and many's the good arf-pint I 'ad to refuse because that little imitation monkey was sitting in the office drawing faces on 'is blotting-paper. But sometimes it don't matter 'ow careful you are, you make a mistake.

"There was a little steamer, called the *Eastern Monarch,* used to come up here in them days, once a week. Fat little tub she was, with a crew o' fattish old men, and a skipper that I didn't like. He'd been in the coasting trade all 'is life, while I've knocked about all over the world, but to hear 'im talk you'd think he knew more about things than I did.

"'Eddication, Bill,' he ses one evening, 'that's the thing! You can't argufy without it; you only talk foolish, like you are doing now.'

" 'There's eddication and there's common sense,' I ses. 'Some people 'as one and some people 'as the other. Give me common sense.'

" 'That's wot you want,' he ses, nodding.

" 'And, o' course,' I ses, looking at 'im, 'there's some people 'asn't got either one or the other.'

"The office-boy came out of the office afore he could think of an answer, and the pair of 'em stood there talking to show off their cleverness, till their tongues ached. I took up my broom and went on sweeping, and they was so busy talking long words they didn't know the meaning of to each other that they was arf choked with dust afore they noticed it. When they did notice it they left off using long words, and the skipper tried to hurt my feelings with a few short ones 'e knew.

" 'It's no good wasting your breath on 'im,' ses the boy. 'You might as well talk to a beer-barrel.'

The Substitute

"He went off, dusting 'imself down with his little pocket-'ankercher, and arter the skipper 'ad told me wot he'd like to do, only he was too sorry for me to do it, 'e went back to the ship to put on a clean collar, and went off for the evening.

"He always used to go off by hisself of a evening, and I used to wonder 'ow he passed the time. Then one night I found out.

"I had just come out of the Bear's Head, and stopped to look round afore going back to the wharf, when I see a couple o' people standing on the swing-bridge saying 'Good-bye' to each other. One of 'em was a man and the other wasn't.

" 'Evening, cap'n,' I ses, as he came towards me, and gave a little start. 'I didn't know you 'ad brought your missis up with you this trip.'

" 'Evening, Bill,' he ses, very peaceful. 'Wot a lovely evening!'

" 'Bee-utiful!' I ses.

" 'So fresh,' ses the skipper, sniffing in some of the air.

" 'Makes you feel quite young agin,' I ses.

The Substitute

"He didn't say nothing to that, except to look at me out of the corner of 'is eye; and stepping on to the wharf had another look at the sky to admire it, and then went aboard his ship. If he 'ad only stood me a pint, and trusted me, things might ha' turned out different.

"Quite by chance I happened to be in the Bear's Head a week arterwards, and, quite by chance, as I came out I saw the skipper saying 'Good-bye' on the bridge agin. He seemed to be put out about something, and when I said 'Wot a lovely evening it would be if only it wasn't raining 'ard!' he said something about knocking my 'ead off.

" 'And you keep your nose out o' my bisness,' he ses, very fierce.

" 'Your bisness!' I ses. 'Wot bisness?'

" 'There's some people as might like to know that you leave the wharf to look arter itself while you're sitting in a pub swilling gallons and gallons o' beer,' he ses, in a nasty sort o' way. 'Live and let live, that's my motter.'"

The Substitute

" 'I don't know wot you're talking about,' I ses, 'but it don't matter anyways. I've got a clear conscience; that's the main thing. I'm as open as the day, and there's nothing about me that I'd mind anybody knowing. Wot a pity it is everybody can't say the same!'

"I didn't see 'im saying 'Good-bye' the next week or the week arter that either, but the third week, arter just calling in at the Bear's Head, I strolled on casual-like and got as far as the bottom of Tower Hill afore I remembered myself. Turning the corner, I a'most fell over the skipper, wot was right in the fair way, shaking 'ands with his lady-friend under the lamp-post. Both of 'em started, and I couldn't make up my mind which gave me the most unpleasant look.

" 'Peep-bo!' I ses, cheerful-like.

"He stood making a gobbling noise at me, like a turkey.

" 'Give me quite a start, you did,' I ses. 'I didn't dream of you being there.'

The Substitute

" 'Get off!' he ses, spluttering. 'Get off, afore I tear you limb from limb! 'Ow dare you follow me about and come spying round corners at me? Wot d'ye mean by it?'

"I stood there with my arms folded acrost my chest, as calm as a cucumber. The other party stood there watching us, and wot 'e could 'ave seen in her, I can't think. She was dressed more like a man than a woman, and it would have taken the good looks of twenty like her to 'ave made one barmaid. I stood looking at 'er like a man in a dream.

" 'Well, will you know me agin?' she ses, in a nasty cracked sort of voice.

" 'I could pick you out of a million,' I ses— 'if I wanted to.'

" 'Clear out!' ses the skipper. 'Clear out! And thank your stars there's a lady present.'

" 'Don't take no notice of 'im, Captain Pratt,' ses the lady. 'He's beneath you. You only encourage people like that by taking notice of 'em. Good-bye.'

"She held out her 'and, and while the skipper

The Substitute

was shaking it I began to walk back to the wharf. I 'adn't gorn far afore I heard 'im coming up behind me, and next moment 'e was walking alongside and saying things to try and make me lose my temper.

" 'Ah, it's a pity your pore missis can't 'ear you!' I ses. 'I expect she thinks you are stowed away in your bunk dreaming of 'er, instead of saying things about a face as don't belong to you.'

" 'You mind your bisness,' he ses, shouting. 'And not so much about my missis! D'ye hear? Wot's it got to do with you? Who asked you to shove your oar in?'

" 'You're quite mistook,' I ses, very calm. 'I'd no idea that there was anything on as shouldn't be. I was never more surprised in my life. If anybody 'ad told me, I shouldn't 'ave believed 'em. I couldn't. Knowing you, and knowing 'ow respectable you 'ave always purtended to be, and also and likewise that you ain't no chicken——'

"I thought 'e was going to 'ave a fit. He

The Substitute

'opped about, waving his arms and stuttering and going on in such a silly way that I didn't like to be seen with 'im. Twice he knocked my 'at off, and arter telling him wot would 'appen if 'e did it agin, I walked off and left him.

"Even then 'e wasn't satisfied, and arter coming on to the wharf and following me up and down like a little dog, he got in front of me and told me some more things he 'ad thought of.

" 'If I catch you spying on me agin,' he ses, 'you'll wish you'd never been born!'

" 'You get aboard and 'ave a quiet sleep,' I ses. 'You're wandering in your mind.'

" 'The lady you saw me with,' he ses, looking at me very fierce, 'is a friend o' mine that I meet sometimes for the sake of her talk.'

" 'Talk!' I ses, staring at 'im. 'Talk! Wot, can't *one* woman talk enough for you? Is your missis dumb? or wot?'

" 'You don't understand,' he ses, cocking up 'is nose at me. 'She's a interleckshal

The Substitute

woman; full of eddication and information.
When my missis talks, she talks about the price
o' things and says she must 'ave more money.
Or else she talks about things I've done, or
sometimes things I 'aven't done. It's all one
to her. There's no pleasure in that sort o'
talk. It don't *help* a man.'

" 'I never 'eard of any talk as did,' I ses.

" 'I don't suppose you did,' he ses, sneering-
like. 'Now, to-night, fust of all, we talked
about the House of Lords and whether it ought
to be allowed; and arter that she gave me quite
a little lecture on insecks.'

" 'It don't seem proper to me,' I ses. 'I
'ave spoke to my wife about 'em once or twice,
but I should no more think of talking about
such things to a single lady——'

"He began to jump about agin as if I'd bit
'im, and he 'ad so much to say about my 'ed
and blocks of wood that I pretty near lost my
temper. I should ha' lost it with some men,
bue 'e was a very stiff-built chap and as hard as
nails.

The Substitute

" 'Beer's your trouble,' he ses, at last. 'Fust of all you put it down, and then it climbs up and soaks wot little brains you've got. Wot you want is a kind friend to prevent you from getting it.'

"I don't know wot it was, but I 'ad a sort of sinking feeling inside as 'e spoke, and next evening, when I saw 'im walk to the end of the jetty with the office-boy and stand there talking to 'im with his 'and on his shoulder, it came on worse than ever. And I put two and two together when the guv'nor came up to me next day, and, arter talking about 'dooty' and 'ow easy it was to get night-watchmen, mentioned in 'a off-'and sort of way that, if I left the wharf at all between six and six, I could stay away altogether.

"I didn't answer 'im a word. I might ha' told 'im that there was plenty of people arter me ready to give me double the money, but I knew he could never get anybody to do their dooty by the wharf like I 'ad done, so I kept quiet. It's the way I treat my missis nowa-

The Substitute

days, and it pays; in the old days I used to waste my breath answering 'er back.

"I wouldn't ha' minded so much if it 'adn't ha' been for that boy. He used to pass me, as 'e went off of a evening, with a little sly smile on 'is ugly little face, and sometimes when I was standing at the gate he'd give a sniff or two and say that he could smell beer, and he *supposed* it came from the Bear's Head.

"It was about three weeks arter the guv'nor 'ad forgot 'imself, and I was standing by the gate one evening, when I saw a woman coming along carrying a big bag in her 'and. I 'adn't seen 'er afore, and when she stopped in front of me and smiled I was on my guard at once. I don't smile at other people, and I don't expect them to smile at me.

" 'At last!' she ses, setting down 'er bag and giving me another smile. 'I thought I was never going to get 'ere."

"I coughed and backed inside a little bit on to my own ground. I didn't want to 'ave that little beast of a office-boy spreading tales about me.

" 'I've come up to 'ave a little fling,' she ses, smiling away harder than ever. 'My husband don't know I'm 'ere. He thinks I'm at 'ome.'

"I think I went back pretty near three yards.

" 'I come up by train,' she ses, nodding.

" 'Yes,' I ses, very severe, 'and wot about going back by it?'

" 'Oh, I shall go back by ship,' she ses. 'Wot time do you expect the *Eastern Monarch* up?'

" 'Well,' I ses, 'ardly knowing wot to make of 'er, 'she ought to be up this tide; but there's no reckoning on wot an old washtub with a engine like a sewing-machine inside 'er will do.'

" 'Oh, indeed!' she ses, leaving off smiling very sudden. 'Oh, indeed! My husband might 'ave something to say about that.'

" 'Your 'usband?' I ses.

" 'Captain Pratt,' she ses, drawing 'erself up. 'I'm Mrs. Pratt. He left yesterday morning, and I've come up 'ere by train to give 'im a little surprise.'

The Substitute

"You might ha' knocked me down with a feather, and I stood there staring at her with my mouth open, trying to think.

" 'Take care,' I ses at last. 'Take care as you don't give 'im too *much* of a surprise!'

" 'Wot do you mean?' she ses, firing up.

" 'Nothing,' I ses. 'Nothing, only I've known 'usbands in my time as didn't like being surprised—that's all. If you take my advice, you'll go straight back home agin.'

" 'I'll tell 'im wot you say,' she ses, 'as soon as 'is ship comes in.'

"That's a woman all over; the moment they get into a temper they want to hurt somebody; and I made up my mind at once that, if anybody was going to be 'urt, it wasn't me. And, besides, I thought it might be for the skipper's good—in the long run.

"I broke it to her as gentle as I could. I didn't tell 'er much, I just gave her a few 'ints. Just enough to make her ask for more.

" 'And mind,' I ses, '*I* don't want to be brought into it. If you should 'appen to take

The Substitute

a fancy into your 'ed to wait behind a pile of empties till the ship comes in, and then slip out and foller your 'usband and give 'im the little surprise you spoke of, it's nothing to do with me.'

" 'I understand,' she ses, biting her lip. 'There's no need for 'im to know that I've been on the wharf at all.'

"I gave 'er a smile—I thought she deserved it—but she didn't smile back. She was rather a nice-looking woman in the ordinary way, but I could easy see 'ow temper spoils a woman's looks. She stood there giving little shivers and looking as if she wanted to bite somebody.

" 'I'll go and hide now,' she ses.

" 'Not yet,' I ses. 'You'll 'ave to wait till that little blackbeetle in the office 'as gorn.'

" 'Blackbeetle?' she ses, staring.

" 'Office-boy,' I ses. 'He'd better not see you at all. S'pose you go off for a bit and come back when I whistle?'

"Afore she could answer the boy came out of the office, ready to go 'ome. He gave a little

The Substitute

bit of a start when 'e saw me talking to a lady, and then 'e nips down sudden, about a couple o' yards away, and begins to do 'is bootlace up. It took 'im some time, because he 'ad to undo it fust, but 'e finished it at last, and arter a quick look at Mrs. Pratt, and one at me that I could ha' smacked his 'ed for, 'e went off whistling and showing 'is little cuffs.

"I stepped out into the road and watched 'im out o' sight. Then I told Mrs. Pratt to pick up 'er bag and foller me.

"As it 'appened there was a big pile of empties in the corner of the ware'ouse wall, just opposite the *Eastern Monarch's* berth. It might ha' been made for the job, and, arter I 'ad tucked her away behind and given 'er a box to sit on, I picked up my broom and began to make up for lost time.

"She sat there as quiet as a cat watching a mouse'ole, and I was going on with my work, stopping every now and then to look and see whether the *Monarch* was in sight, when I 'appened to turn round and see the office-boy

225

standing on the edge of the wharf with his back to the empties, looking down at the water. I nearly dropped my broom.

" ''Ullo!' I ses, going up to 'im. 'I thought you 'ad gorn 'ome.'

" 'I was going,' he ses, with a nasty oily little smile, 'and then it struck me all of a sudden 'ow lonely it was for you *all alone 'ere*, and I come back to keep you company.'

"He winked at something acrost the river as 'e spoke, and I stood there thinking my 'ardest wot was the best thing to be done. I couldn't get Mrs. Pratt away while 'e was there; besides which I felt quite sartain she wouldn't go. The only 'ope I 'ad was that he'd get tired of spying on me and go away before he found out she was 'iding on the wharf.

"I walked off in a unconcerned way—not too far—and, with one eye on 'im and the other on where Mrs. Pratt was 'iding, went on with my work. There's nothing like 'ard work when a man is worried, and I was a'most forgetting

The Substitute

my troubles, when I looked up and saw the *Monarch* coming up the river.

"She turned to come into 'er berth, with the skipper shouting away on the bridge and making as much fuss as if 'e was berthing a liner. I helped to make 'er fast, and the skipper, arter 'e had 'ad a good look round to see wot 'e could find fault with, went below to clean 'imself.

"He was up agin in about ten minutes, with a clean collar and a clean face, and a blue necktie that looked as though it 'ad got yeller measles. Good temper 'e was in, too, and arter pulling the office-boy's ear, gentle, as 'e was passing, he stopped for a moment to 'ave a word with 'im.

" 'Bit late, ain't you?' he ses.

" 'I've been keeping a eye on the watchman,' ses the boy. 'He works better when 'e knows there's somebody watching 'im.'

" 'Look 'ere!' I ses. 'You take yourself off; I've had about enough of you. You take your little face 'ome and ask your mother to wipe its

The Substitute

nose. Strickly speaking, you've no right to be on the wharf at all at this time.'

" 'I've as much right as other people,' he ses, giving me a wicked look. 'I've got more right than some people, p'r'aps.'

"He stooped down deliberate and, picking up a bit o' coke from the 'eap by the crane, pitched it over at the empties.

" 'Stop that!' I ses, shouting at 'im.

" 'What for?' 'e ses, shying another piece. 'Why shouldn't I?'

" ' 'Cos I won't 'ave it,' I ses. 'D'ye hear? Stop it!'

"I rushed at 'im as he sent another piece over, and for the next two or three minutes 'e was dodging me and chucking coke at the empties, with the fool of a skipper standing by laughing, and two or three of the crew leaning over the side and cheering 'im on.

" 'All right,' he ses, at last, dusting 'is hands together. 'I've finished. There's no need to make such a fuss over a bit of coke.'

" 'You've wasted pretty near arf a 'undered-

The Substitute

weight,' I ses. 'I've a good mind to report you.'

" 'Don't do that, watchman!' he ses, in a pitiful voice. 'Don't do that! 'Ere, I tell you wot I'll do. I'll pick it all up agin.'

"Afore I could move 'and or foot he 'ad shifted a couple o' cases out of 'is way and was in among the empties. I stood there dazed-like while two bits o' coke came flying back past my 'ed; then I 'eard a loud whistle, and 'e came out agin with 'is eyes rolling and 'is mouth wide open.

" 'Wot's the matter?' ses the skipper, staring at 'im.

" 'I—I—I'm sorry, watchman,' ses that beast of a boy, purtending 'e was 'ardly able to speak. 'I'd no idea——'

" 'All right,' I ses, very quick.

" 'Wot's the matter?' ses the skipper agin; and as 'e spoke it came over me like a flash wot a false persition I was in, and wot a nasty-tempered man 'e could be when 'e liked.

" 'Why didn't you tell me you'd got a lady-friend there?' ses the boy, shaking his 'ed at me. 'Why, I might 'ave hit 'er with a bit o' coke, and never forgiven myself!'

" '*Lady-friend!*' ses the skipper, with a start. 'Oh, Bill, I *am* surprised!'

"My throat was so dry I couldn't 'ardly speak. 'It's my missis,' I ses, at last.

" 'Your missis?' ses the skipper. 'Wot's she 'iding behind there for?'

" 'She—she's shy,' I ses. 'Always was, all 'er life. She can't bear other people. She likes to be alone with me.'

" 'Oh, watchman!' ses the boy. 'I wonder where you expect to go to?'

" 'Missis my grandmother!' ses the skipper, with a wink. 'I'm going to 'ave a peep.'

" 'Stand back!' I ses, pushing 'im off. 'I don't spy on you, and I don't want you to come spying on me. You get off! D'ye hear me? Get off!'

"We had a bit of a struggle, till my foot slipped, and while I was waving my arms and trying to get my balance back 'e made a dash

The Substitute

for the empties. Next moment he was roaring like a mad bull that 'ad sat down in a sorsepan of boiling water, and rushing back agin to kill me.

"I believe that if it 'adn't ha' been for a couple o' lightermen wot 'ad just come on to the jetty from their skiff, and two of his own 'ands, he'd ha' done it. Crazy with passion 'e was, and it was all the four of 'em could do to hold 'im. Every now and then he'd get a yard nearer to me, and then they'd pull 'im back a couple o' yards and beg of 'im to listen to reason and 'ear wot I 'ad to say. And as soon as I started and began to tell 'em about 'is lady-friend he broke out worse than ever. People acrost the river must ha' wondered wot was 'appening. There was two lightermen, two sailormen, me and the skipper, and Mrs. Pratt all talking at once, and nobody listening but the office-boy. And in the middle of it all the wicket was pushed open and the 'ed of the lady wot all the trouble was about peeped in, and drew back agin.

The Substitute

" 'There you are !' I ses, shouting my 'ardest. 'There she is. That's the lady I was telling you about. Now, then: put 'em face to face and clear my character. Don't let 'er escape.'

"One o' the lightermen let go o' the skipper and went arter 'er, and, just as I was giving the other three a helping 'and, 'e came back with 'er. Mrs. Pratt caught 'er breath, and as for the skipper, 'e didn't know where to look, as the saying is. I just saw the lady give 'im one quick look, and then afore I could dream of wot was coming, she rushes up to me and flings 'er long, bony arms round my neck.

" 'Why, William !' she ses, 'wot's the matter? Why didn't you meet me? Didn't you get my letter? Or 'ave you ceased to care for me ?"

" 'Let go !' I ses, struggling. 'Let go ! D'ye 'ear? Wot d'ye mean by it? You've got 'old of the wrong one.'

" 'Oh, William !' she ses, arf strangling me. ' 'Ow can you talk to me like that? Where's your 'art ?'

"I never knew a woman so strong. I don't

The Substitute

suppose she'd ever 'ad the chance of getting 'er arms round a man's neck afore, and she hung on to me as if she'd never let go. And all the time I was trying to explain things to them over 'er shoulder I could see they didn't believe a word I was saying. One o' the lightermen said I was a 'wonder,' and the other said I was a 'fair cough-drop.' *Me!*

"She got tired of it at last, but by that time I was so done up I couldn't say a word. I just dropped on to a box and sat there getting my breath back while the skipper forgave 'is wife for 'er unjust suspicions of 'im—but told 'er not to do it agin—and the office-boy was saying I'd surprised even 'im. The last I saw of the lady-friend, the two lightermen was helping 'er to walk to the gate, and the two sailormen was follering 'er up behind, carrying 'er pocket-'ankercher and upberella."

Striking Hard

Striking Hard

"YOU'VE what?" demanded Mrs. Porter, placing the hot iron carefully on its stand and turning a heated face on the head of the family.

"Struck," repeated Mr. Porter; "and the only wonder to me is we've stood it so long as we have. If I was to tell you all we've 'ad to put up with I don't suppose you'd believe me."

"Very likely," was the reply. "You can keep your fairy-tales for them that like 'em. They're no good to me."

"We stood it till flesh and blood could stand it no longer," declared her husband, "and at last we came out, shoulder to shoulder, singing. The people cheered us, and one of our leaders made 'em a speech."

"I should have liked to 'ave heard the singing," remarked his wife. "If they all sang like you, it must ha' been as good as a pantermime!

Striking Hard

Do you remember the last time you went on strike?"

"This is different," said Mr. Porter, with dignity.

"All our things went, bit by bit," pursued his wife, "all the money we had put by for a rainy day, and we 'ad to begin all over again. What are we going to live on? O' course, you might earn something by singing in the street; people who like funny faces might give you something! Why not go upstairs and put your 'ead under the bed-clothes and practise a bit?"

Mr. Porter coughed. "It'll be all right," he said, confidently. "Our committee knows what it's about; Bert Robinson is one of the best speakers I've ever 'eard. If we don't all get five bob a week more I'll eat my 'ead."

"It's the best thing you could do with it," snapped his wife. She took up her iron again, and turning an obstinate back to his remarks resumed her work.

Mr. Porter lay long next morning, and, dressing with comfortable slowness, noticed with

Striking Hard

pleasure that the sun was shining. Visions of a good breakfast and a digestive pipe, followed by a walk in the fresh air, passed before his eyes as he laced his boots. Whistling cheerfully he went briskly downstairs.

It was an October morning, but despite the invigorating chill in the air the kitchen-grate was cold and dull. Herring-bones and a disorderly collection of dirty cups and platters graced the table. Perplexed and angry, he looked around for his wife, and then, opening the back-door, stood gaping with astonishment. The wife of his bosom, who should have had a bright fire and a good breakfast waiting for him, was sitting on a box in the sunshine, elbows on knees and puffing laboriously at a cigarette.

"Susan!" he exclaimed.

Mrs. Porter turned, and, puffing out her lips, blew an immense volume of smoke. "Halloa!" she said, carelessly.

"Wot—wot does this mean?" demanded her husband.

Mrs. Porter smiled with conscious pride. "I

Striking Hard

made it come out of my nose just now," she replied. "At least, some of it did, and I swallowed the rest. Will it hurt me?"

"Where's my breakfast?" inquired the other, hotly. "Why ain't the kitchen-fire alight? Wot do you think you're doing of?"

"I'm not doing anything," said his wife, with an aggrieved air. "I'm on strike."

Mr. Porter reeled against the door-post. "*Wot!*" he stammered. "On strike? Nonsense! You can't be."

"O, yes, I can," retorted Mrs. Porter, closing one eye and ministering to it hastily with the corner of her apron. "Not 'aving no Bert Robinson to do it for me, I made a little speech all to myself, and here I am."

She dropped her apron, replaced the cigarette, and, with her hands on her plump knees, eyes him steadily.

"But—but this ain't a factory," objected the dismayed man; "and, besides — *I won't 'ave it!*"

240

Striking Hard

Mrs. Porter laughed—a fat, comfortable laugh, but with a touch of hardness in it.

"All right, mate," she said, comfortably. "What are you out on strike for?"

"Shorter hours and more money," said Mr. Porter, glaring at her.

His wife nodded. "So am I," she said. "I wonder who gets it first?"

She smiled agreeably at the bewildered Mr. Porter, and, extracting a paper packet of cigarettes from her pocket, lit a fresh one at the stub of the first.

"That's the worst of a woman," said her husband, avoiding her eye and addressing a sanitary dustbin of severe aspect; "they do things without thinking first. That's why men are superior; before *they* do a thing they look at it all round, and upside down, and—and—make sure it can be done. Now, you get up in a temper this morning, and the first thing you do—not even waiting to get my breakfast ready first—is to go on strike. If you'd thought for two minutes you'd see as 'ow it's impossible fcr

Striking Hard

you to go on strike for more than a couple of hours or so."

"Why?" inquired Mrs. Porter.

"Kids," replied her husband, triumphantly. "They'll be coming 'ome from school soon, won't they? And they'll be wanting their dinner, won't they?"

"That's all right," murmured the other, vaguely.

"After which, when night comes," pursued Mr. Porter, "they'll 'ave to be put to bed. In the morning they'll 'ave to be got up and washed and dressed and given their breakfast and sent off to school. Then there's shopping wot must be done, and beds wot must be made."

"I'll make ours," said his wife, decidedly. "For my own sake."

"And wot about the others?" inquired Mr. Porter.

"The others'll be made by the same party as washes the children, and cooks their dinner for 'em, and puts 'em to bed, and cleans the 'ouse," was the reply.

Striking Hard

"I'm not going to have your mother 'ere," exclaimed Mr. Porter, with sudden heat. "Mind that!"

"I don't want her," said Mrs. Porter. "It's a job for a strong, healthy man, not a pore old thing with swelled legs and short in the breath."

"Strong—'ealthy—man!" repeated her husband, in a dazed voice. "Strong—'eal—— Wot are you talking about?"

Mrs. Porter beamed on him. "You," she said, sweetly.

There was a long silence, broken at last by a firework display of expletives. Mrs. Porter, still smiling, sat unmoved.

"You may smile!" raved the indignant Mr. Porter. "You may sit there smiling and smoking like a—like a man, but if you think that I'm going to get the meals ready, and soil my 'ands with making beds and washing-up, you're mistook. There's some 'usbands I know as would set about you!"

Mrs. Porter rose. "Well, I can't sit here

243

gossiping with you all day," she said, entering the house.

"Wot are you going to do?" demanded her husband, following her.

"Going to see Aunt Jane and 'ave a bit o' dinner with her," was the reply. "And after that I think I shall go to the 'pictures.' If you 'ave bloaters for dinner be very careful with little Jemmy and the bones."

"I forbid you to leave this 'ouse!" said Mr. Porter, in a thrilling voice. "If you do you won't find nothing done when you come home, and all the kids dirty and starving."

"Cheerio!" said Mrs. Porter.

Arrayed in her Sunday best she left the house half an hour later. A glance over her shoulder revealed her husband huddled up in a chair in the dirty kitchen, gazing straight before him at the empty grate.

He made a hearty breakfast at a neighbouring coffee-shop, and, returning home, lit the fire and sat before it, smoking. The return of the four children from school, soon after midday,

found him still wrestling with the difficulties of
the situation. His announcement that their
mother was out and that there would be no dinner was received at first in stupefied silence.
Then Jemmy, opening his mouth to its widest
extent, acted as conductor to an all-too-willing
chorus.

The noise was unbearable, and Mr. Porter
said so. Pleased with the tribute, the choir re-
doubled its efforts, and Mr. Porter, vociferat-
ing orders for silence, saw only too clearly the
base advantage his wife had taken of his affec-
tion for his children. He took some money
from his pocket and sent the leading treble out
marketing, after which, with the assistance of a
soprano aged eight, he washed up the breakfast
things and placed one of them in the dustbin.

The entire family stood at his elbow as he
cooked the dinner, and watched, with bated
breath, his frantic efforts to recover a sausage
which had fallen out of the frying-pan into the
fire. A fourfold sigh of relief heralded its
return to the pan.

Striking Hard

"Mother always —— " began the eldest boy.

Mr. Porter took his scorched fingers out of his mouth and smacked the critic's head.

The dinner was not a success. Portions of half-cooked sausages returned to the pan, and coming back in the guise of cinders failed to find their rightful owners.

"Last time we had sausages," said the eight-year-old Muriel, "they melted in your mouth."

Mr. Porter glowered at her.

"Instead of in the fire," said the eldest boy, with a mournful snigger.

"If I get up to you, my lad," said the harassed Mr. Porter, "you'll know it! Pity you don't keep your sharpness for your lessons! Wot country is Africa in?"

"Why, Africa's a continent!" said the startled youth.

"Jes so," said his father; "but wot I'm asking you is: wot country is it in?"

"Asia," said the reckless one, with a side-glance at Muriel.

Striking Hard

"And why couldn't you say so before?" demanded Mr. Porter, sternly. "Now, you go to the sink and give yourself a thorough good wash. And mind you come straight home from school. There's work to be done."

He did some of it himself after the children had gone, and finished up the afternoon with a little shopping, in the course of which he twice changed his grocer and was threatened with an action for slander by his fishmonger. He returned home with his clothes bulging, although a couple of eggs in the left-hand coat-pocket had done their best to accommodate themselves to his figure.

He went to bed at eleven o'clock, and at a quarter past, clad all too lightly for the job, sped rapidly downstairs to admit his wife.

"Some 'usbands would 'ave let you sleep on the doorstep all night," he said, crisply.

"I know they would," returned his wife, cheerfully. "That's why I married *you*. I remember the first time I let you come 'ome with me, mother ses: 'There ain't much of

Striking Hard

'im, Susan,' she ses; 'still, arf a loaf is better than ——' "

The bedroom-door slammed behind the indignant Mr. Porter, and the three lumps and a depression which had once been a bed received his quivering frame again. With the sheet obstinately drawn over his head he turned a deaf ear to his wife's panegyrics on striking and her heartfelt tribute to the end of a perfect day. Even when standing on the cold floor while she remade the bed he maintained an attitude of unbending dignity, only relaxing when she smote him light-heartedly with the bolster. In a few ill-chosen words he expressed his opinion of her mother and her deplorable methods of bringing up her daughters.

He rose early next morning, and, after getting his own breakfast, put on his cap and went out, closing the street-door with a bang that awoke the entire family and caused the somnolent Mrs. Porter to open one eye for the purpose of winking with it. Slowly, as became a man of leisure, he strolled down to the works, and, moving from knot to knot of his colleagues, discussed the prospects of victory. Later on, with a little natural diffidence, he drew Mr. Bert Robinson apart and asked his advice upon a situation which was growing more and more difficult.

"I've got my hands pretty full as it is, you know," said Mr. Robinson, hastily.

"I know you 'ave, Bert," murmured the other. "But, you see, she told me last night she's going to try and get some of the other chaps' wives to join 'er, so I thought I ought to tell you."

Mr. Robinson started. "Have you tried giving her a hiding?" he inquired.

Mr. Porter shook his head. "I daren't trust myself," he replied. "I might go too far, once I started."

"What about appealing to her better nature?" inquired the other.

"She ain't got one," said the unfortunate.

"Well, I'm sorry for you," said Mr. Robinson, "but I'm busy. I've got to see a Labour-

Striking Hard

leader this afternoon, and two reporters, and this evening there's the meeting. Try kindness first, and if that don't do, lock her up in her bedroom and keep her on bread and water."

He moved off to confer with his supporters, and Mr. Porter, after wandering aimlessly about for an hour or two, returned home at midday with a faint hope that his wife might have seen the error of her ways and provided dinner for him. He found the house empty and the beds unmade. The remains of breakfast stood on the kitchen-table, and a puddle of cold tea decorated the floor. The arrival of the children from school, hungry and eager, completed his discomfiture.

For several days he wrestled grimly with the situation, while Mrs. Porter, who had planned out her week into four days of charing, two of amusement, and Sunday in bed, looked on with smiling approval. She even offered to give him a little instruction—verbal—in scrubbing the kitchen-floor.

Striking Hard

Mr. Porter, who was on his knees at the time, rose slowly to his full height, and, with a superb gesture, emptied the bucket, which also contained a scrubbing-brush and lump of soap, into the back-yard. Then he set off down the street in quest of a staff.

He found it in the person of Maudie Stevens, aged fourteen, who lived a few doors lower down. Fresh from school the week before, she cheerfully undertook to do the housework and cooking, and to act as nursemaid in her spare time. Her father, on his part, cheerfully undertook to take care of her wages for her, the first week's, payable in advance, being banked the same evening at the Lord Nelson.

It was another mouth to feed, but the strike-pay was coming in very well, and Mr. Porter, relieved from his unmanly tasks, walked the streets a free man. Beds were made without his interference, meals were ready (roughly) at the appointed hour, and for the first time since the strike he experienced satisfaction in finding fault with the cook. The children's content was not so great, Maudie possessing a faith in the virtues of soap and water that they made no attempt to share. They were greatly relieved when their mother returned home after spending a couple of days with Aunt Jane.

"What's all this?" she demanded, as she entered the kitchen, followed by a lady-friend.

"What's all what?" inquired Mr. Porter, who was sitting at dinner with the family.

"That," said his wife, pointing at the cook-general.

Mr. Porter put down his knife and fork. "I got 'er in to help," he replied, uneasily.

"Do you hear that?" demanded his wife, turning to her friend, Mrs. Gorman. "Oh, these masters!"

"Ah!" said her friend, vaguely.

"A strike-breaker!" said Mrs. Porter, rolling her eyes.

"Shame!" said Mrs. Gorman, beginning to understand.

"Coming after my job, and taking the bread out of my mouth," continued Mrs. Porter, fluently. "Underselling me too, I'll be bound. That's what comes of not having pickets."

"Unskilled labour," said Mrs. Gorman, tightening her lips and shaking her head.

"A scab!" cried Mrs. Porter, wildly. "A scab!"

"Put her out," counselled her friend.

"Put her out!" repeated Mrs. Porter, in a terrible voice. "Put her out! I'll tear her limb from limb! I'll put her in the copper and boil her!"

Her voice was so loud and her appearance so alarming that the unfortunate Maudie, emitting three piercing shrieks, rose hastily from the table and looked around for a way of escape. The road to the front-door was barred, and with a final yelp that set her employer's teeth on edge she dashed into the yard and went home *viâ* the back-fences. Housewives busy in their kitchens looked up in amazement at the spectacle of a pair of thin black legs descending one fence, scudding across the yard to the accompaniment of a terrified moaning, and scrambling

Striking Hard

madly over the other. At her own back-door
Maudie collapsed on the step, and, to the in-
tense discomfort and annoyance of her father,
had her first fit of hysterics.

"And the next scab that comes into my house
won't get off so easy," said Mrs. Porter to her
husband. "D'you understand?"

"If you 'ad some husbands——" began Mr.
Porter, trembling with rage.

"Yes, I know," said his wife, nodding.
"Don't cry, Jemmy," she added, taking the
youngest on her knee. "Mother's only having
a little game. She and dad are both on strike
for more pay and less work."

Mr. Porter got up, and without going
through the formality of saying good-bye to the
hard-featured Mrs. Gorman, put on his cap and
went out. Over a couple of half-pints taken as
a sedative, he realized the growing seriousness
of his position.

In a dull resigned fashion he took up his
household duties again, made harder now than
before by the scandalous gossip of the ag-

254

Striking Hard

grieved Mr. Stevens. The anonymous present of a much-worn apron put the finishing touch to his discomfiture; and the well-meant offer of a fair neighbour to teach him how to shake a mat without choking himself met with a reception that took her breath away.

It was a surprise to him one afternoon to find that his wife had so far unbent as to tidy up the parlour. Ornaments had been dusted and polished and the carpet swept. She had even altered the position of the furniture. The table had been pushed against the wall, and the easy-chair, with its back to the window, stood stiffly confronting six or seven assorted chairs, two of which at least had been promoted from a lower sphere.

"It's for the meeting," said Muriel, peeping in.

"Meeting?" repeated her father, in a dazed voice.

"Strike-meetings," was the reply. "Mrs. Gorman and some other ladies are coming at four o'clock. Didn't mother tell you?"

Striking Hard

Mr. Porter, staring helplessly at the row of chairs, shook his head.

"Mrs. Evans is coming," continued Muriel, in a hushed voice—"the lady what punched Mr. Brown because he kept Bobbie Evans in one day. He ain't been kept in since. I wish you——"

She stopped suddenly, and, held by her father's gaze, backed slowly out of the room. Mr. Porter, left with the chairs, stood regarding them thoughtfully. Their emptiness made an appeal that no right-minded man could ignore. He put his hand over his mouth and his eyes watered.

He spent the next half-hour in issuing invitations, and at half-past three every chair was filled by fellow-strikers. Three cans of beer, clay pipes, and a paper of shag stood on the table. Mr. Benjamin Todd, an obese, fresh-coloured gentleman of middle age, took the easy-chair. Glasses and teacups were filled.

"Gentlemen," said Mr. Todd, lighting his pipe, "afore we get on to the business of this meeting I want to remind you that there is another meeting, of ladies, at four o'clock; so we've got to hurry up. O' course, if it should happen that we ain't finished——"

"Go on, Bennie!" said a delighted admirer.

"I see a female 'ead peeping in at the winder already," said a voice.

"Let 'em peep," said Mr. Todd, benignly. "Then p'r'aps they'll be able to see how to run a meeting."

"There's two more 'eads," said the other. "Oh, Lord, I know I sha'n't be able to keep a straight face!"

"*H'sh!*" commanded Mr. Todd, sternly, as the street-door was heard to open. "Be'ave yourself. As I was saying, the thing we've got to consider about this strike——"

The door opened, and six ladies, headed by Mrs. Porter, entered the room in single file and ranged themselves silently along the wall.

"Strike," proceeded Mr. Todd, who found himself gazing uneasily into the eyes of Mrs. Gorman—"strike—er—strike——"

Striking Hard

"He said that before," said a stout lady, in a loud whisper; "I'm sure he did."

"Is," continued Mr. Todd, "that we have got to keep this—this—er——"

"Strike," prompted the same voice.

Mr. Todd paused, and, wiping his mouth with a red pocket-handkerchief, sat staring straight before him.

"I move," said Mrs. Evans, her sharp features twitching with excitement, "that Mrs. Gorman takes the chair."

" 'Ow can I take it when he's sitting in it?" demanded that lady.

"She's a lady that knows what she wants and how to get it," pursued Mrs. Evans, unheeding. "She understands men——"

"I've buried two 'usbands," murmured Mrs. Gorman, nodding.

"And how to manage them," continued Mrs. Evans. "I move that Mrs. Gorman takes the chair. Those in favour——"

Mr. Todd, leaning back in his chair and grip-

Striking Hard

ping the arms, gazed defiantly at a row of palms.

"Carried unanimously!" snapped Mrs. Evans.

Mrs. Gorman, tall and bony, advanced and stood over Mr. Todd. Strong men held their breath.

"It's my chair," she said, gruffly. "I've been moved into it."

"Possession," said Mr. Todd, in as firm a voice as he could manage, "is nine points of the law. I'm here and——"

Mrs. Gorman turned, and, without the slightest warning, sat down suddenly and heavily in his lap. A hum of admiration greeted the achievement.

"Get up!" shouted the horrified Mr. Todd. "Get up!"

Mrs. Gorman settled herself more firmly.

"Let *me* get up," said Mr. Todd, panting.

Mrs. Gorman rose, but remained in a hovering position, between which and the chair Mr. Todd, flushed and dishevelled, extricated himself in all haste. A shrill titter of laughter and a clapping of hands greeted his appearance. He turned furiously on the pallid Mr. Porter.

"What d'you mean by it?" he demanded. "Are you the master, or ain't you? A man what can't keep order in his own house ain't fit to be called a man. If my wife was carrying on like this——"

"I wish I was your wife," said Mrs. Gorman, moistening her lips.

Mr. Todd turned slowly and surveyed her.

"I don't," he said, simply, and, being by this time near the door, faded gently from the room.

"Order!" cried Mrs. Gorman, thumping the arm of her chair with a large, hard-working fist. "Take your seats, ladies."

A strange thrill passed through the bodies of her companions and communicated itself to the men in the chairs. There was a moment's tense pause, and then the end man, muttering something about "going to see what had happened to poor old Ben Todd," rose slowly and went out. His companions, with heads erect and a

Striking Hard

look of cold disdain upon their faces, followed him.

It was Mr. Porter's last meeting, but his wife had several more. They lasted, in fact, until the day, a fortnight later, when he came in with flushed face and sparkling eyes to announce that the strike was over and the men victorious.

"Six bob a week more!" he said, with enthusiasm. "You see, I was right to strike, after all."

Mrs. Porter eyed him. "I am out for *four* bob a week more," she said, calmly.

Her husband swallowed. "You—you don't understand 'ow these things are done," he said, at last. "It takes time. We ought to ne-ne-gotiate."

"All right," said Mrs. Porter, readily. "Seven shillings a week, then."

"Let's say four and have done with it," exclaimed the other, hastily.

And Mrs. Porter said it.

Dirty Work

Dirty Work

IT was nearly high-water, and the night-watchman, who had stepped aboard a lighter lying alongside the wharf to smoke a pipe, sat with half-closed eyes enjoying the summer evening. The bustle of the day was over, the wharves were deserted, and hardly a craft moved on the river. Perfumed clouds of shag, hovering for a time over the lighter, floated lazily towards the Surrey shore.

"There's one thing about my job," said the night-watchman, slowly, "it's done all alone by yourself. There's no foreman a-hollering at you and offering you a penny for your thoughts, and no mates to run into you from behind with a loaded truck and then ask you why you didn't look where you're going to. From six o'clock in the evening to six o'clock next morning I'm my own master."

Dirty Work

He rammed down the tobacco with an experienced forefinger and puffed contentedly.

People like you 'ud find it lonely (he continued, after a pause); I did at fust. I used to let people come and sit 'ere with me of an evening talking, but I got tired of it arter a time, and when one chap fell overboard while 'e was showing me 'ow he put his wife's mother in 'er place, I gave it up altogether. There was three foot o' mud in the dock at the time, and arter I 'ad got 'im out, he fainted in my arms.

Arter that I kept myself to myself. Say wot you like, a man's best friend is 'imself. There's nobody else'll do as much for 'im, or let 'im off easier when he makes a mistake. If I felt a bit lonely I used to open the wicket in the gate and sit there watching the road, and p'r'aps pass a word or two with the policeman. Then something 'appened one night that made me take quite a dislike to it for a time.

I was sitting there with my feet outside, smoking a quiet pipe, when I 'eard a bit of a noise in the distance. Then I 'eard people running and

266

Dirty Work

shouts of "Stop, thief!" A man came along round the corner full pelt, and, just as I got up, dashed through the wicket and ran on to the wharf. I was arter 'im like a shot and got up to 'im just in time to see him throw something into the dock. And at the same moment I 'eard the other people run past the gate.

"Wot's up?" I ses, collaring 'im.

"Nothing," he ses, breathing 'ard and struggling. "Let me go."

He was a little wisp of a man, and I shook 'im like a dog shakes a rat. I remembered my own pocket being picked, and I nearly shook the breath out of 'im.

"And now I'm going to give you in charge," I ses, pushing 'im along towards the gate.

"Wot for?" he ses, purtending to be surprised.

"Stealing," I ses.

"You've made a mistake," he ses; "you can search me if you like."

"More use to search the dock," I ses. "I see you throw it in. Now you keep quiet, else you'll get 'urt. If you get five years I shall be all the more pleased."

I don't know 'ow he did it, but 'e did. He seemed to sink away between my legs, and afore I knew wot was 'appening, I was standing upside down with all the blood rushing to my 'ead. As I rolled over he bolted through the wicket, and was off like a flash of lightning.

A couple o' minutes arterwards the people wot I 'ad 'eard run past came back agin. There was a big fat policeman with 'em—a man I'd seen afore on the beat—and, when they 'ad gorn on, he stopped to 'ave a word with me.

" 'Ot work," he ses, taking off his 'elmet and wiping his bald 'ead with a large red handkerchief. "I've lost all my puff."

"Been running?" I ses, very perlite.

"Arter a pickpocket," he ses. "He snatched a lady's purse just as she was stepping aboard the French boat with her 'usband. 'Twelve pounds in it in gold, two peppermint lozenges, and a postage stamp.' "

Dirty Work

He shook his 'ead, and put his 'elmet on agin.

"Holding it in her little 'and as usual," he ses. "Asking for trouble, I call it. I believe if a woman 'ad one hand off and only a finger and thumb left on the other, she'd carry 'er purse in it."

He knew a'most as much about wimmen as I do. When 'is fust wife died, she said 'er only wish was that she could take 'im with her, and she made 'im promise her faithful that 'e'd never marry agin. His second wife, arter a long illness, passed away while he was playing hymns on the concertina to her, and 'er mother, arter looking at 'er very hard, went to the doctor and said she wanted an inquest.

He went on talking for a long time, but I was busy doing a bit of 'ead-work and didn't pay much attention to 'im. I was thinking o' twelve pounds, two lozenges, and a postage stamp laying in the mud at the bottom of my dock, and arter a time 'e said 'e see as 'ow I was waiting

to get back to my night's rest, and went off—
stamping.

I locked the wicket when he 'ad gorn away,
and then I went to the edge of the dock and
stood looking down at the spot where the purse
'ad been chucked in. The tide was on the ebb,
but there was still a foot or two of water atop
of the mud. I walked up and down, thinking.

I thought for a long time, and then I made
up my mind. If I got the purse and took it to
the police-station, the police would share the
money out between 'em, and tell me they 'ad
given it back to the lady. If I found it and put
a notice in the newspaper—which would cost
money—very likely a dozen or two ladies would
come and see me and say it was theirs. Then
if I gave it to the best-looking one and the one
it belonged to turned up, there'd be trouble.
My idea was to keep it—for a time—and then
if the lady who lost it came to me and asked
me for it I would give it to 'er.

Once I had made up my mind to do wot was
right I felt quite 'appy, and arter a look up and

Dirty Work

down, I stepped round to the Bear's Head and 'ad a couple o' goes o' rum to keep the cold out. There was nobody in there but the landlord, and 'e started at once talking about the thief, and 'ow he 'ad run arter him in 'is shirt-sleeves.

"My opinion is," he ses, "that 'e bolted on one of the wharves and 'id 'imself. He disappeared like magic. Was that little gate o' yours open?"

"I was on the wharf," I ses, very cold.

"You might ha' been on the wharf and yet not 'ave seen anybody come on," he ses, nodding.

"Wot d'ye mean?" I ses, very sharp.

"Nothing," he ses. "Nothing."

"Are you trying to take my character away?" I ses, fixing 'im with my eye.

"Lo' bless me, no!" he ses, staring at me. "It's no good to me."

He sat down in 'is chair behind the bar and went straight off to sleep with his eyes screwed up as tight as they would go. Then 'e opened

Dirty Work

his mouth and snored till the glasses shook. I suppose I've been one of the best customers he ever 'ad, and that's the way he treated me. For two pins I'd ha' knocked 'is ugly 'ead off, but arter waking him up very sudden by dropping my glass on the floor I went off back to the wharf.

I locked up agin, and 'ad another look at the dock. The water 'ad nearly gone and the mud was showing in patches. My mind went back to a sailorman wot had dropped 'is watch overboard two years before, and found it by walking about in the dock in 'is bare feet. He found it more easy because the glass broke when he trod on it.

The evening was a trifle chilly for June, but I've been used to roughing it all my life, especially when I was afloat, and I went into the office and began to take my clothes off. I took off everything but my pants, and I made sure o' them by making braces for 'em out of a bit of string. Then I turned the gas low, and, arter slipping on my boots, went outside.

Dirty Work

It was so cold that at fust I thought I'd give up the idea. The longer I stood on the edge looking at the mud the colder it looked, but at last I turned round and went slowly down the ladder. I waited a moment at the bottom, and was just going to step off when I remembered that I 'ad got my boots on, and I 'ad to go up agin and take 'em off.

I went down very slow the next time, and anybody who 'as been down an iron ladder with thin, cold rungs, in their bare feet, will know why, and I had just dipped my left foot in, when the wharf-bell rang.

I 'oped at fust that it was a runaway-ring, but it kept on, and the longer it kept on, the worse it got. I went up that ladder agin and called out that I was coming, and then I went into the office and just slipped on my coat and trousers and went to the gate.

"Wot d'you want?" I ses, opening the wicket three or four inches and looking out at a man wot was standing there.

"Are you old Bill?" he ses.

Dirty Work

"I'm the watchman," I ses, sharp-like. "Wot d'you want?"

"Don't bite me!" he ses, purtending to draw back. "I ain't done no 'arm. I've come round about that glass you smashed at the Bear's Head."

"Glass!" I ses, 'ardly able to speak.

"Yes, glass," he ses—"thing wot yer drink out of. The landlord says it'll cost you a tanner, and 'e wants it now in case you pass away in your sleep. He couldn't come 'imself cos he's got nobody to mind the bar, so 'e sent me. Why! Halloa! Where's your boots? Ain't you afraid o' ketching cold?"

"You clear off," I ses, shouting at him. "D'ye 'ear me? Clear off while you're safe, and you tell the landlord that next time 'e insults me I'll smash every glass in 'is place and then sit 'im on top of 'em! Tell 'im if 'e wants a tanner out o' me, to come round 'imself, and see wot he gets."

It was a silly thing to say, and I saw it arterwards, but I was in such a temper I 'ardly knew

Dirty Work

wot I *was* saying. I slammed the wicket in 'is
face and turned the key and then I took off my
clothes and went down that ladder agin.

It seemed colder than ever, and the mud when
I got fairly into it was worse than I thought it
could ha' been. It stuck to me like glue, and
every step I took seemed colder than the one
before. 'Owever, when I make up my mind to
do a thing, I do it. I fixed my eyes on the
place where I thought the purse was, and every
time I felt anything under my foot I reached
down and picked it up—and then chucked it
away as far as I could so as not to pick it up
agin. Dirty job it was, too, and in five minutes
I was mud up to the neck, a'most. And I 'ad
just got to wot I thought was the right place,
and feeling about very careful, when the bell
rang agin.

I thought I should ha' gorn out o' my mind.
It was just a little tinkle at first, then another
tinkle, but, as I stood there all in the dark and
cold trying to make up my mind to take no notice of it, it began to ring like mad. I 'ad to

go—I've known men climb over the gate afore now—and I didn't want to be caught in that dock.

The mud seemed stickier than ever, but I got out at last, and, arter scraping some of it off with a bit o' stick, I put on my coat and trousers and boots just as I was and went to the gate, with the bell going its 'ardest all the time.

When I opened the gate and see the landlord of the Bear's Head standing there I turned quite dizzy, and there was a noise in my ears like the roaring of the sea. I should think I stood there for a couple o' minutes without being able to say a word. I could think of 'em.

"Don't be frightened, Bill," ses the landlord. "I'm not going to eat you."

"He looks as if he's walking in 'is sleep," ses the fat policeman, wot was standing near by. "Don't startle 'im."

"He always looks like that," ses the landlord.

I stood looking at 'im. I could speak then, but I couldn't think of any words good enough;

Dirty Work

not with a policeman standing by with a note-book in 'is pocket.

"Wot was you ringing my bell for?" I ses, at last.

"Why didn't you answer it before?" ses the landlord. "D'you think I've got nothing better to do than to stand ringing your bell for three-quarters of an hour? Some people would report you."

"I know my dooty," I ses; "there's no craft up to-night, and no reason for anybody to come to my bell. If I was to open the gate every time a parcel of overgrown boys rang my bell I should 'ave enough to do."

"Well, I'll overlook it this time, seeing as you're an old man and couldn't get another sleeping-in job," he ses, looking at the police-man for him to see 'ow clever 'e was. "Wot' about that tanner? That's wot I've come for."

"You be off," I ses, starting to shut the wicket. "You won't get no tanner out of me."

"All right," he ses, "I shall stand here and go on ringing the bell till you pay up, that's all."

Dirty Work

He gave it another tug, and the policeman instead of locking 'im up for it stood there laughing.

I gave 'im the tanner. It was no use standing there arguing over a tanner, with a purse of twelve quid waiting for me in the dock, but I told 'im wot people thought of 'im.

"Arf a second, watchman," ses the policeman, as I started to shut the wicket agin. "You didn't see anything of that pickpocket, did you?"

"I did not," I ses.

" 'Cos this gentleman thought he might 'ave come in here," ses the policeman.

" 'Ow could he 'ave come in here without me knowing it?" I ses, firing up.

"Easy," ses the landlord, "and stole your boots into the bargain."

"He might 'ave come when your back was turned," ses the policeman, "and if so, he might be 'iding there now. I wonder whether you'd mind me having a look round?"

"I tell you he ain't 'ere," I ses, very short,

Dirty Work

"but, to ease your mind, I'll 'ave a look round myself arter you've gorn."

The policeman shook his 'ead. "Well, o' course, I can't come in without your permission," he ses, with a little cough, "but I 'ave an idea, that if it was your guv'nor 'ere instead of you he'd ha' been on'y too pleased to do anything 'e could to help the law. I'll beg his pardon tomorrow for asking you, in case he might object."

That settled it. That's the police all over, and that's 'ow they get their way and do as they like. I could see 'im in my mind's eye talking to the guv'nor, and letting out little things about broken glasses and such-like by accident. I drew back to let 'im pass, and I was so upset that when that little rat of a landlord follered 'im I didn't say a word.

I stood and watched them poking and prying about the wharf as if it belonged to 'em, with the light from the policeman's lantern flashing about all over the place. I was shivering with cold and temper. The mud was drying on me, and I couldn't 'elp noticing the smell of it. Nobody could. And wot was worse than all was, that the tide 'ad turned and was creeping over the mud in the dock.

They got tired of it at last and came back to where I was and stood there shaking their 'eads at me.

"If he was on the wharf 'e must 'ave made his escape while you was in the Bear's Head," ses the policeman.

"He *was* in my place a long time," ses the landlord.

"Well, it's no use crying over spilt milk," ses the policeman. "Funny smell about 'ere, ain't there?" he ses, sniffing, and turning to the landlord. "Wot is it?"

"I dunno," ses the landlord. "I noticed it while we was talking to 'im at the gate. It seems to foller 'im about."

"I've smelt things I like better," ses the policeman, sniffing agin. "It's just like the foreshore when somebody 'as been stirring the mud up a bit."

Dirty Work

"If you've finished 'unting for the pickpocket I'll let you out and get on with my work," I ses, drawing myself up.

"Good night," ses the policeman, moving off.

"Good night, dear," ses the landlord. "Mind you tuck yourself up warm."

I lost my temper for the moment and afore I knew wot I was doing I 'ad got hold of him and was shoving 'im towards the gate as 'ard as I could shove. He pretty near got my coat off in the struggle, and next moment the policeman 'ad turned his lantern on me and they was both staring at me as if they couldn't believe their eyesight.

"He—he's turning black!" ses the landlord.

"He's turned black!" ses the policeman.

They both stood there looking at me with their mouths open, and then afore I knew wot he was up to, the policeman came close up to me and scratched my chest with his finger-nail.

"It's mud!" he ses.

"You keep your nails to yourself," I ses. "It's nothing to do with you."

Dirty Work

"Unless it's a case of 'tempted suicide," he ses, looking at me very 'ard.

"Ah!" ses the landlord.

"There's no mud on 'is clothes," ses the policeman, looking me over with his lantern agin.

"He must 'ave gone in naked, but I should like to see 'is legs to make—All right! All right! Keep your 'air on."

"You look arter your own legs, then," I ses, very sharp, "and mind your own business."

"It is my business," he ses, turning to the landlord. "Was 'e strange in his manner at all when 'e was in your place to-night?"

"He smashed one o' my best glasses," ses the landlord.

"So he did," ses the policeman. "So he did. I'd forgot that. Do you know 'im well?"

"Not more than I can 'elp," ses the landlord. "He's been in my place a good bit, but I never knew of any reason why 'e should try and do away with 'imself. If he's been disappointed in love, he ain't told me anything about it."

I suppose that couple o' fools 'ud 'ave stood

Dirty Work

there talking about me all night if I'd ha' let 'em, but I had about enough of it.

"Look 'ere," I ses, "you're very clever, both of you, but you needn't worry your 'eads about me. I've just been having a mud-bath, that's all."

"A *mud-bath!*" ses both of 'em, squeaking like a couple o' silly parrots.

"For rheumatics," I ses. "I 'ad it something cruel to-night, and I thought that p'r'aps the mud 'ud do it good. I read about it in the papers. There's places where you pay pounds and pounds for 'em, but, being a pore man, I 'ad to 'ave mine on the cheap."

The policeman stood there looking at me for a moment, and then 'e began to laugh till he couldn't stop 'imself.

"Love-a-duck!" he ses, at last, wiping his eyes. "I wish I'd seen it."

"Must ha' looked like a fat mermaid," ses the landlord, wagging his silly 'ead at me. "I can just see old Bill sitting in the mud a-combing his 'air and singing."

Dirty Work

They 'ad some more talk o' that sort, just to show each other 'ow funny they was, but they went off at last, and I fastened up the gate and went into the office to clean myself up as well as I could. One comfort was they 'adn't got the least idea of wot I was arter, and I 'ad a fancy that the one as laughed last would be the one as got that twelve quid.

I was so tired that I slept nearly all day arter I 'ad got 'ome, and I 'ad no sooner got back to the wharf in the evening than I see that the landlord 'ad been busy. If there was one silly fool that asked me the best way of making mud-pies, I should think there was fifty. Little things please little minds, and the silly way some of 'em went on made me feel sorry for my sects.

By eight o'clock, 'owever, they 'ad all sheered off, and I got a broom and began to sweep up to 'elp pass the time away until low-water. On'y one craft 'ad come up that day—a ketch called the *Peewit*—and as she was berthed at the end of the jetty she wasn't in my way at all.

Dirty Work

Her skipper came on to the wharf just afore ten. Fat, silly old man 'e was, named Fogg. Always talking about 'is 'ealth and taking medicine to do it good. He came up to me slow like, and, when 'e stopped and asked me about the rheumatics, the broom shook in my 'and.

"Look here," I ses, "if you want to be funny, go and be funny with them as likes it. I'm fair sick of it, so I give you warning."

"Funny?" he ses, staring at me with eyes like a cow. "Wot d'ye mean? There's nothing funny about rheumatics; I ought to know; I'm a martyr to it. Did you find as 'ow the mud did you any good?"

I looked at 'im—hard, but 'e stood there looking at me with his fat baby-face, and I knew he didn't mean any harm; so I answered 'im perlite and wished 'im good night.

"I've 'ad pretty near everything a man can have," he ses, casting anchor on a empty box, "but I think the rheumatics was about the worst of 'em all. I even tried bees for it once."

"Bees!" I ses. *"Bees!"*

Dirty Work

"Bee-stings," he ses. "A man told me that if I could on'y persuade a few bees to sting me, that 'ud cure me. I don't know what 'e meant by persuading! they didn't *want* no persuading. I took off my coat and shirt and went and rocked one of my neighbour's bee-hives next door, and I thought my last hour 'ad come."

He sat on that box and shivered at the memory of it.

"Now I take Dr. Pepper's pellets instead," he ses. "I've got a box in my state-room, and if you'd like to try 'em you're welcome."

He sat there talking about the complaints he had 'ad and wot he 'ad done for them till I thought I should never have got rid of 'im. He got up at last, though, and, arter telling me to always wear flannel next to my skin, climbed aboard and went below.

I knew the hands was aboard, and arter watching 'is cabin-skylight until the light was out, I went and undressed. Then I crept back on to the jetty, and arter listening by the *Peewit*

Dirty Work

to make sure that they was all asleep, I went back and climbed down the ladder.

It was colder than ever. The cold seemed to get into my bones, but I made up my mind to 'ave that twelve quid if I died for it. I trod round and round the place where I 'ad seen that purse chucked in until I was tired, and the rubbish I picked up by mistake you wouldn't believe.

I suppose I 'ad been in there arf an hour, and I was standing up with my teeth clenched to keep them from chattering, when I 'appened to look round and see something like a white ball coming down the ladder. My 'art seemed to stand still for a moment, and then it began to beat as though it would burst. The white thing came down lower and lower, and then all of a sudden it stood in the mud and said, "Ow!"

"Who is it?" I ses. "Who are you?"

"Halloa, Bill!" it ses. "Ain't it perishing cold?"

It was the voice o' Cap'n Fogg, and if ever

Dirty Work

I wanted to kill a fellow-creetur, I wanted to then.

" 'Ave you been in long, Bill?" he ses.

"About ten minutes," I ses, grinding my teeth.

"Is it doing you good?" he ses.

I didn't answer 'im.

"I was just going off to sleep," he ses, "when I felt a sort of hot pain in my left knee. O' course, I knew what it meant at once, and instead o' taking some of the pellets I thought I'd try your remedy instead. It's a bit nippy, but I don't mind that if it does me good."

He laughed a silly sort o' laugh, and then I'm blest if 'e didn't sit down in that mud and waller in it. Then he'd get up and come for'ard two or three steps and sit down agin.

"Ain't you sitting down, Bill?" he ses, arter a time.

"No," I ses, "I'm not."

"I don't think you can expect to get the full benefit unless you do," he ses, coming up close

Dirty Work

to me and sitting down agin. "It's a bit of a shock at fust, but—— Halloa!"

"Wot's up?" I ses.

"Sitting on something hard," he ses. "I wish people 'ud be more careful."

He took a list to port and felt under the starboard side. Then he brought his 'and up and tried to wipe the mud off and see wot he 'ad got.

"Wot is it?" I ses, with a nasty sinking sort o' feeling inside me.

"I don't know," he ses, going on wiping. "It's soft outside and 'ard inside. It——"

"Let's 'ave a look at it," I ses, holding out my 'and.

"It's nothing," he ses, in a queer voice, getting up and steering for the ladder. "Bit of oyster-shell, I think."

He was up that ladder hand over fist, with me close behind 'im, and as soon as he 'ad got on to the wharf started to run to 'is ship.

"Good night, Bill," he ses, over 'is shoulder.

"Arf a moment." I ses, follering 'im.

Dirty Work

"I must get aboard," he ses; "I believe I've got a chill," and afore I could stop 'im he 'ad jumped on and run down to 'is cabin.

I stood on the jetty for a minute or two, trembling all over with cold and temper. Then I saw he 'ad got a light in 'is cabin, and I crept aboard and peeped down the skylight. And I just 'ad time to see some sovereigns on the table, when he looked up and blew out the light.

www.ingramcontent.com/pod-product-compliance
Lightning Source LLC
Chambersburg PA
CBHW030936260626
47169CB00002B/497